THE
GAME COCK
and other stories

by

MICHAEL McLAVERTY

with illustrations by

SISTER IRENA UPTEGROVE, O. S. B.

New Yor̶
THE DEVIN-ADA[
1948

First Printing June, 1947
Second Printing July, 1947
Third Printing February 1948

Designed by Peter Döblin

PRINTED IN UNITED STATES OF AMERICA

To
GERTRUDE GAFFNEY

301634

Contents

Contents

The Game Cock

WHEN I was young we came to Belfast and my father kept a game cock and a few hens. At the back of the street was waste ground where the fowl could scrape, and my father built a shed for them in the yard and sawed a hole in the back door so that they could hop in and out as they took the notion. In the mornings our cock was always first out on the waste ground.

We called him Dick, but he was none of your ordinary cocks, for he had a pedigree as long as your arm, and his grandfather and grandmother were of Indian breed. He was lovely to look at, with his long yellow legs, black glossy feathers in the chest and tail, and reddish streaky neck. In the long summer evenings my father would watch him for hours, smiling at the way he tore the clayey ground with his claws, coming on a large earwig, and calling the hens to share it. But one day when somebody lamed him with a stone, my father grew so sad that he couldn't take his supper.

We had bought him from Jimmy Reilly, the blind man, and many an evening he came to handle him. I would be doing my school exercise at the kitchen table, my father, in his shirt sleeves, reading the paper. A knock would come to the door, and with great expectancy in his voice my father'd say, "That's the men now. Let them in, son."

And when I opened the door I'd say, "Mind the step!" and in

would shuffle wee Johnny Moore leading the blind man. They'd
sit on the sofa; Jimmy Reilly, hat on head, and two fists clasped
round the shank of the walking stick between his legs; and
Johnny Moore with a stinking clay pipe in his mouth.

As soon as they started the talk I'd put down my pen and
listen to them.

"Sit up to the fire, men, and get a bit of the heat."

"That's a snorer of a fire you've on, Mick," would come from
the blind man.

"What kind of coals is them?" says Johnny Moore, for he had
my father pestered with questions.

"The best English; them's none of your Scotch slates!"

"And what's the price of them a ton?"

"They cost a good penny," my father would answer crossly.

"And where do you get them?"

The blind man's stick would rattle on the kitchen tiles and
he'd push out his lower lip, stroke his beard and shout, "They're
good coals, anyway, no matter where they're got." And then
add in his slow natural voice. "How's the cock, Mick?"

"He's in great fettle, Jimmy. He's jumping out of his pelt."
And he'd tell how the comb was reddening and how he had
chased Maguire's dunghill of a rooster from about the place.
And the blind man would smile and say, "That's the stuff! He'll
soon have the walk to himself; other cocks would annoy him."

With a lighted candle I would be sent out to the yard to lift
Dick off the roost. The roosts were low so that the cock wouldn't
bruise his feet when flying to the ground. He'd blink his eyes
and cluck-cluck in his throat when I'd bring him into the gaslight and hand him to the blind man.

Jimmy fondled him like a woman fondling a cat. He gently
stroked the neck and tail, and then stretched out one wing and

THE GAME COCK
AND OTHER STORIES

then the other. "He's in great condition. We could cut his comb
and wattles any time and have him ready for Easter." And he'd
put him down on the tiles and listen to the scrape of his claws.
Then he'd feel the muscles on the thighs, and stick out his
beard with joy, "There's no coldness about that fella, Mick.
He has shoulders on him as broad as a bulldog. Aw, my lovely
fella," feeling the limber of him as his claws pranced on the
tiles. "He'll do us credit. A hould you he'll win a main."

My father would stuff his hands in his pockets and rise off
his heels, "And you think he's doing well, Jimmy?"

"Hould yer tongue, man, I wish I was half as fit," Jimmy
would answer, his sightless eyes raised to the ceiling.

And one evening as they talked like this about the cock and
forthcoming fights, Johnny Moore sneaked across to the table
and gave me sums out of his head: *A ropemaker made a rope
for his marrying daughter, and in the rope he made twenty
knots and in each knot he put a purse, and in each purse he put
seven three-penny bits and nine half-pennies. How much of a
dowry did the daughter get?*

I couldn't get the answer and he took the pipe from his mouth
and laughed loudly, "The scholars, nowadays, have soft brains.
You can't do it with your pencil and paper and an old man like
me can do it in my head."

My face burned as I said, "But we don't learn them kind of
sums." He laughed so much that I was glad when it was time
for him to lead the blind man home.

A few evenings afterwards they were back again; the blind
man with special scissors to cut Dick's comb and wattles.
Jimmy handed the scissors to my father, then he held the cock,
his forefinger in its mouth and his thumb at the back of its head.

"Now, Mick," said he, "try and cut it with one stroke."

When my sisters saw the chips of comb snipped off with the scissors and the blood falling on the tiles they began to cry, "That's a sin, father! That's a sin!"

"Tush, tush," said my father, and the blood on his sleeves. "He doesn't feel it. It's just like getting your hair cut. Isn't that right, Jimmy?"

"That's right; just like getting your toenails cut."

But when Dick clucked and shook his head with pain, my sisters cried louder and were sent out to play, and I went into the scullery to gather cobwebs to stop the bleeding.

In a few days the blood had hardened and Dick was his old self again. The men came nearly every night and talked about the cock fights to be held near Toome at Easter. They made plans for Dick's training and arranged how he was to be fed.

About a fortnight before the fights my father got a long box and nailed loose sacking over the front to keep it in darkness. Dick was put into this and his feathers and tail were clipped. For the first two days he got no feed so as to keep his weight down. Then we gave him hard-boiled eggs, but they didn't agree with him and made him scour. The blind man recommended a strict diet of barley and barley water. "That's the stuff to keep his nerves strong and his blood up. A hould you it'll not scour him."

Every morning we took him from his dark box and gave him a few runs up and down the yard. Johnny Moore had made a red flannel bag stuffed with straw, and Dick sparred at this daily, and when he had finished my father would lift him in his arms, stroke him gently, and sponge the feet and head. Day by day the cock grew peevish, and once when he nebbed at me I gave him a clout that brought my father running to the yard.

The night before the fights the steel spurs were tied on him to see how he would look in the pit. "Ah, Jimmy, if you could

see him," said my father to the blind man. "He's the picture of health."

The blind man fingered his beard and putting a hand in his pocket, took out a few pound notes and spat on them for luck. "Put that on him to-morrow. There's not another cock this side of the Bann nor in all County Derry that could touch him." Even Johnny Moore risked a few shillings, and the next morning before five o'clock my father wakened me to go to Toome.

It was Easter Monday and there were no trams running early so we set off to walk to the Northern Counties Railway to catch the half-six train. The cock was in a potato bag under my arm, and I got orders not to squeeze him, while my father carried the overcoats and a gladstone filled with things for my Granny, who lived near the place where the cocks were to fight.

The streets were deserted, and our feet echoed in the chill air. Down the Falls Road we hurried. The shopblinds were pulled down, the tram lines shining, and no smoke coming from the chimneys. At the Public Baths my father looked at his watch and then stood out in the road to see the exact time by the Baths' clock.

"Boys-a-boys, my watch is slow. We'll need to hurry." In the excitement the cock got his neb out and pecked at me. I dropped the bag, and out jumped the cock and raced across the tram lines, the two of us after him.

"Don't excite him, son. Take him gently." We tried to corner him in a doorway, my father with his hand out-stretched calling in his sweetest way, "Dick, Dick, Dicky." But as soon as he stooped to lift him, the cock dived between his legs, and raced up North Howard Street, and stood contemplating a dark-green public lavatory.

"Whisht," said my father, holding my arm as I went to go forward. "Whisht! If he goes in there we'll nab him."

The cock stood, head erect, and looked up and down the bare street. Then he scraped each side of his bill on the step of the lavatory and crowed into the morning.

"Man, but that's the brazen tinker of a cock for you," said my father, looking at his watch. And then, as if Dick were entering the hen-shed, in he walked, and in after him tiptoed my father, and out by the roofless top flew the cock with a few feathers falling from him.

I swished him off the top and he flew for all he was worth over the tram lines, down Alma Street and up on a yard wall.

"We'll be late for the train if we don't catch him quick, and maybe have the peelers down on us before we know where we are."

Up on the wall I was heaved and sat with legs astride. The cock walked away from me, and a dog in the yard yelped and jumped up the back door.

"I'm afraid, Da, I'm afraid."

"Come down out of that and don't whinge there."

A baby started to cry and a man looked out of a window and shouted, "What the hell's wrong?"

"We're after a cock," replied my father apologetically.

The man continued to lean out of the window in his shirt, and a woman yelled from the same room, "Throw a bucket of water round them, Andy. A nice time of the morning to be chasing a bloody rooster."

Here and there a back door opened and barefooted men in their shirts and trousers came into the entry. They all chased after Dick.

"Ah, easy, easy," said my father to a man who was swiping at

Dick savagely with a yard-brush. "Don't hit him with that."

By this time the cock had walked half way down the entry, still keeping to the top of the yard walls. Women shouted and dogs barked, and all the time I could hear my father saying, "If we don't catch him quick we'll miss the train."

"Aw," said one man, looking at the scaldy appearance of the cock. "Sure he's not worth botherin' about. There's not as much on him as'd set a rat-trap."

My father kept silent about Dick's pedigree for he didn't want anyone to know about the cockfights, and maybe have the police after us.

We had now reached the end of the entry and Dick flew off the wall and under a little handcart that stood in a corner. Five men bunched in after him, and screeching and scolding the cock was handed to my father.

"I can feel his heart going like a traction engine," he said, when we were on the road again. "He'll be bate. The blind man's money and everybody's money will be lost. Lost!"

We broke into a trot, I carrying the gladstone, and my father the cock and the overcoats. Along York Street we raced, gazing up at the big clocks and watching the hands approach half-six. Sweat broke out on us and a stitch came in my side, but I said nothing as I lagged behind trying to keep pace.

We ran into the station and were just into the carriage when out went the train.

"Aw-aw-aw," said my father, sighing out all his breath in one puff. "I'm done. Punctured! That's a nice start for an Easter Monday!"

He took off his hard hat and pulled out a handkerchief. His bald head was speckled with sweat and the hat had made a red groove on his brow. He puffed and ah-ee-d so many times I thought he'd faint, and I sat with my heart thumping, my shirt clammy with sweat, waiting with fear for what he'd say. But he didn't scold me.

"It was my own fault," he said. "I should have tied a bit of string round the neck of the bag. He'll be bate! He'll be bate!"

He took the spurs from his pocket and pulled the corks off the steel points. "I might as well strap them on a jackdaw as put them on Dick this day, for he'll be tore asunder after that performance."

As the train raced into the country we saw the land covered with a thin mist, and ploughed fields with shining furrows. The cold morning air came into the carriage; it was lovely and fresh. My father's breathing became quieter, and he even pointed out farms that would make great "walks" for cocks. It was going to be a grand day: a foggy sun was bursting through, and crows flew around trees that were laden with their nests.

Dick was taken from the bag and petted; and then my father stretched himself out on the seat and fell asleep. I watched the telegraph wires rising and falling, and kept a lookout for the strange birds that were cut out in the hedge near Doagh.

When we came to Toome my father tied the neck of the bag with a handkerchief and sent me on in front for fear the police might suspect something. The one-streeted village was shady and cool, the sun skimming the housetops. Pieces of straw littered the road, and a few hens stood at the closed barrack door, their droppings on the doorstep.

We passed quickly through the silent village and turned on to the long country road that led to my Granny's. Behind us the train rumbled and whistled over the bridge; and then across the still country came the dull cheer of the Bann waterfall and the wind astir in the leafing branches. Once my father told me to sit and rest myself while he crossed a few fields to a white cottage. It wasn't long until he was back again. "I've got the stuff in my pocket that'll make him gallop. The boys in Lough Beg made a run of poteen for Easter."

When we reached my Granny's she was standing at the door, a string garter fallen round her ankle, and a basin in her hand; near her my Uncle's bicycle was turned upside down and he was mending a puncture. They had great welcome for us and smiled when my father put the poteen on the table. He took tumblers from the dresser, filled one for my Granny, and in another he softened a few pieces of bread for the cock.

My Granny sat at the fire and at every sip she sighed and held the glass up to the light. "Poor fellas, but they run great risks to make that. None of your ould treacle about the Lough Beg stuff . . . made from the best of barley."

As she sipped it she talked to me about my school, and the little sense my father had in his head to be bothering himself about game cocks and maybe land himself in jail; and when the car came up for him she went to the door and waved him off. "Mind the peelers," she shouted. "Ye'd never know where they'd be sniffing around."

During the day I played about the house and tormented the tethered goat, making her rise on her hind legs. I went to the well at the foot of the field and carried a bucket of water to my Granny, and she said I was a big, strong man. Later my Uncle brought me through the tumbled demesne wall and showed me where he had slaughtered a few trees for the fire. I talked to him about Dick and I asked him why he didn't keep game cocks. He laughed at me and said, "I wouldn't have them about the place. They destroy the hens and make them as wild as the rooks." I didn't talk any more about game cocks, but all the time as we walked to the Big House I thought about Dick and wondered would he win his fights. The Big House was in ruins, crows were nesting in the chimneys, and the lake was covered with rushes and green scum. When I asked my uncle where were all the ladies and gentlemen and the gamekeeper, he spat through the naked windows and replied, "They took the land from the people and God cursed them."

When we came back my Granny was standing at the door looking up and down the road wondering what was keeping my father. A few fellows coming from the cockfights passed on bicycles, and soon my father arrived. He was in great form, his face red, and his navy blue trousers covered with clay.

The cock's comb was scratched with blood, his feathers streaky, and his eyes half shut. He was left in the byre until the tea was over. While my father was taking the tea he got up from the table and stood in the middle of the floor telling how Dick had won his fights. "Five battles he won and gave away weight twice."

"Take your tea, Mick, and you can tell us after," my Granny said, her hands in her sleeves, and her feet tapping the hearth.

He would eat for a few minutes and he'd be up again. "Be the holy frost if ye'd seen him tumbling the big Pyle cock from Derry it'd have done yer heart good. I never seen the like of it. Aw, he's a great battler. And look at the morning he put in on them yard walls . . . up and down a dozen streets he went, running and flying and crowing. And then to win his fights. Wait till Jimmy Reilly hears about this and the nice nest egg I have for him. The poteen was great stuff. A great warrior!" And he smiled in recollection.

I was glad when he was ready for home and gladder still when we were in the train where I made the wheels rumble and chant: . . . *They took the land from the people . . . God cursed them.*

It was dark when we reached Belfast and I carried Dick in the potato bag. We got into a tram at the station; the lights were lit and we sat downstairs. The people were staring at my father, at the clabber on his boots and the wrinkles on his trousers. But he paid no heed to them. In the plate glass opposite I could see our reflections; my father was smiling with his lips together, and I knew he was thinking of the cock.

"He's very quiet, Da," I whispered. "The fightin' has fairly knocked the capers out of him."

"Aw, son, he's a great warrior," and he put his hand in his pocket and slipped me a half crown. "I'll get his photo took as soon as he's his old self again."

I held the money tightly in my hand, and all the way home I rejoiced that Johnny Moore wasn't with us, for he would have set me a problem about a half-crown.

In the kitchen I left the bag on the floor and sat on the sofa, dead tired. My father got down the olive oil to rub on Dick's legs, but when he opened the bag the cock never stirred. He took him out gently and raised his head, but it fell forward limply, and from the open mouth blood dripped to the floor.

"God-a-God, he's dead!" said my father, stretching out one of the wings. He held up the cock's head in the gaslight and looked at him. Then he put him on the table without a word and sat on a chair. For awhile I said nothing, and then I asked quietly, "What'll you do with him, Da?"

He turned and looked at the cock, stretched on the table. "Poor Dick!" he said. And I felt a lump rise in my throat.

Then he got up from the chair. "What'll I do with him! What'll I do with him! I'll get him stuffed! That's what I'll do!"

The White Mare

"WHAT about Paddy, Kate? He'll be raging if we let him lie any longer and it such a brave morning."

"Och, let him rage away, Martha. He'll know his driver before night if he ploughs the field."

"'Deed that's the truth, and with an old mare that's done and dropping off her feet."

"He'll get sense when it's too late. And to hear him gabbling you'd think he was a young man and not the spent old thorn that he is. But what's the use of talking! Give him a call."

Kate, seated on a stool, blew at the fire with the bellows, blew until the flames were spurting madly in and out between the brown sods. Martha waited until the noise of the blazing fire had ceased, and then rapped loudly at the room door off the kitchen. The knocking was answered by a husky voice.

Paddy was awake, sitting up in the bed, scratching his head with his two hands and blinking at the bare window in the room. His face was bony and unshaven, his moustache grey and straggly. Presently he threw aside the blankets and crawled out backwards on to the cold cement floor. He stood at the window. In the early hours of the morning it had rained, but now it was clear. A high wind had combed the white hair of the sky, and on the bare thorn at the side of the byre shivered swollen buds of rain. Across the cobbled street was his stubble field, bounded on one side by a hedge and a hill, and on the other sides by loose stones. Two newly-ploughed furrows ran down the centre and at the top of them lay his plough with a crow swaying nervously on one of the handles. Last evening when the notion took him he had commenced the ploughing, and to-day, with the help of God, he'd finish it. He thought of the rough feel of the handles, the throb of the coulter cutting the clay, and the warm sweaty smell from his labouring mare.

With difficulty he stretched himself to his full height, his bony joints creaking, and his lungs filling with the rain-washed air that came through the open window; he drew in great breaths of it, savouring it as he would savour the water from a spring well. As he was about to turn away, the crow rose up suddenly and flew off. At that moment Kate was crossing to the byre, one hand holding a can, and the other a stick. Paddy watched, trying to divine from her movements the kind of temper she was in this morning. But he noted nothing unusual about her. There was the same active walk, the black triangle of shawl dipping down her back, and the grey head with the man's cap on it. To look at her you wouldn't think she was drawing the pension for over six years. No, there wasn't another house in the whole island with three drawing the pension — not another house! We're a great stock and no mistake; a great pity none of us married!

Kate's voice pierced the air as she shouted at a contrary cow. Oh, a good kind woman, but a tartar when you stirred her. He'd hold his tongue this morning till he had the mare tackled and then they could barge away. Anyway what do women know about a man's job, with their milking cows, and feeding hens, and washing clothes. H'm! a field has to be ploughed and it takes a man to plough it.

When he came from the room Kate was just in from milking and Martha moved slowly about the table arranging the mugs and the farls of bread. Paddy stooped and took his clay-caked boots from below the table. He knew by the look of his sisters that he'd have to lace them himself this morning. It always caused him pain to stoop, but what matter, he'd soon be out in the quiet of the fields where no one would say a word to him.

They all sat at the table together, eating silently and with the slow deliberation that comes with the passing years. Now and again as Paddy softened his bread in the tea, Kate would give him a hard little look. It was coming, he knew it. If only they'd keep silent until he had finished. But it was coming; the air was heavy with stifled talk.

"I suppose you'll do half the field to-day," began Kate.

" 'Deed and I'll do it all," he replied with a touch of hardness in his voice knowing he must be firm.

"Now, Paddy, you should get Jamesy's boys over to help you," said Martha pleadingly.

"Them wee buttons of men! I'd have it done while they'd be thinkin' about it. I wouldn't have them about the place again, with their ordering this and ordering that, and their tea after their dinner, and wanting their pipes filled every minute with good tobacco. I can do it all myself with the help of God. All myself!" and with this he brought his mug down sharply on the table.

"If you get another attack of the pains it's us'll have to suffer," put in Kate, "attending you morning, noon, and night. Have you lost your wits, man! It's too old you're getting and it'd be better if we sold the mare and let the two bits of fields."

Paddy kept silent; it was better to let them fire away.

"The mare's past her day," Kate continued. "It's rest the poor thing wants an' not pulling a plough with a done man behind it."

"Done, is it? There's work in me yet, and I can turn a furrow as straight as anyone in the island. Done! H'm, I've my work to be doing."

He got up, threw his coat across his shoulder, and strode towards the door. His two sisters watched him go out, nodding their heads. "Ah, but that's a foolish, hard-headed man. There's no fool like an old fool!"

Paddy crossed to the stable and the mare nickered when she heard his foot on the cobbled street. Warm, hay-scented air met him as he opened the door. Against the wall stood the white mare. She cocked her ears and turned her head towards the light. She was big and fat with veins criss-crossing on her legs like dead ivy roots on the limbs of a tree. Her eyes were wet-shining and black, their upper lids fringed with long grey lashes. Paddy stroked her neck and ran his fingers through her yellow-grey mane.

A collar with the straw sticking out of it was soon buckled on, and with chains rattling from her sides he led her through the stone-slap into the field. He looked at the sky, at the sea with its patches of mist, and then smilingly went to his plough. Last evening the coulter was cutting too deep and he now adjusted it, giving it a final smack with the spanner that rang out clear in the morning air. The mare was sniffing the rain-wet grass under the hedge and she raised her head jerkily as he approached, sending a shower of cold drops from the bushes down his neck. He shivered, but spoke kindly to the beast as he led her to be tackled. In a few minutes all was ready, and gripping the handles in God's name, he ordered the horse forward, and his day's work began.

The two sisters eyed him from the window. His back was

towards them. Above the small stone fence they could see his
bent figure, his navy-blue trousers with a brown patch on the
seat of them, his grey shirt sleeves, the tattered back of his
waistcoat, and above his shabby hat the swaying quarters of
the mare.

"Did you ever see such a man since God made you! I declare
to goodness he'll kill that mare," said Martha.

"It's himself he'll kill if he's not careful. Let me bold Paddy
be laid up after this and 'tis the last field he'll plough, for I'll
sell the mare, done beast and all as she is!" replied Kate, pressing her face closer to the window.

Paddy was unaware of their talk. His eyes were on the sock
as it slid slowly through the soft earth and pushed the gleaming furrows to the side. He was living his life. What call had he
for help! Was it sit by and look at Jamesy's boys ploughing the
field, and the plough wobbling to and fro like you'd think they
were learning to ride a bicycle.

" 'Way up, girl," he shouted to the mare, " 'way up, Maggie!"
and his veins swelled on his arms as he leant on the handles.
The breeze blowing up from the sea, the cold smell of the
broken clay, and the soft hizzing noise of the plough, all soothed
his mind and stirred him to new life.

As the day advanced the sun rose higher, but there was little
heat from it, and frosty vapours still lingered about the rock-
heads and about the sparse hills. But slowly over the little field
horse and plough still moved, moved like timeless creatures of
the earth, while alongside, their shadows followed on the clay.
Overhead and behind swarmed the gulls, screeching and dart-
ing for the worms, their flitting shadows falling coolly on
Paddy's neck and on the back of the mare. At the end of the
ridge he stopped to take a rest, surveying with pleasure the

number of turned furrows, and wondering if his sisters were proud of him now. He looked up at the house: it was low and whitewashed, one end thatched and the other corrugated. There seemed to be no life about it except the smoke from the chimney and a crow plucking at the thatch. Soon it flew off with a few straws hanging from its bill. It's a pity he hadn't the gun now, he'd soon stop that thief; at nesting-time they wouldn't leave a roof above your head. But to-morrow he'd fix them. He spat on his hands and gripped the handles.

At two o'clock he saw Kate making down at the top of the field and he moved to the hedge. She brought him a few empty sacks to sit on; a good kind girl when you took her the right way. She had the real stuff in the egg-punch too, nothing like it for a working man.

When he had taken his first swig of tea she said quietly, "It's time you were quitting, Paddy."

He must be careful. "Did you see that devil of a crow on the thatch?"

"I didn't, thank God. But I've heard it said that it's the sure sign of a death."

"Did you now?" he replied with a smile. "Isn't that queer, and me always thinking that it was the sign of new life and them nesting."

It's no use trying to frighten him, she thought, no use talking to him; he'll learn his own lesson before morning. Up she got and went off.

"Give the mare a handful of hay and a bucket of water," he called after her.

He lay back, smoking his pipe at his ease, enjoying the look of the ribbed field and the familiar scene. To his right over the stone fence lay the bony rocks stretching their lanky legs into the sea; and now and again he could hear the hard rattle of the pebbles being sucked into the gullet of the waves. Opposite on a jutting headland rose the white column of the East Lighthouse, as lonely-looking as ever. There never was much stir on this side of the island anyway. It was a mile or more from the quay where the little sailing boats went twice a week to Ballycastle. But what little there was of land was good. As he looked down at the moist clay, pressing nail-marks in it with his toe, he pitied the people in the Lower End with their shingly fields and stunted crops. How the news would travel to them to-night about his ploughing! Every mouthful of talk would be about him and the old white mare. He puffed at his pipe vigorously and a sweet smile came over his wrinkled face. Then the shouts of the children coming from school made him aware of the passing time.

He must get up now for the sun would set early. He knocked out his pipe on the heel of his boot. When he made to rise he felt stiff in the shoulders, and a needle of pain jagged one of his legs making him give a silly little laugh. It's a bad thing to sit too long and the day flying. He walked awkwardly over to Maggie, and presently they were going slowly over the field again. The yellow-green bands at each side of the dark clay grew narrower and narrower as each new furrow was turned. Soon they would disappear. The sky was clear and the sun falling; the daylight might hold till he had finished.

The coulter crunched on a piece of delph and its white chips were mosaiced on the clay. "'Man alive, but them's the careless women," he said aloud. "If the mare cut her feet there'd be a quare how-d'ye-do!" At that moment Kate came out to the stone fence and gathered clothes that had been drying. She stood with one hand on her cheek, looking at the slow, almost imperceptible, movement of the plough. She turned, shooshed the hens from her feet, and went in slamming the door behind her.

Over the rock heads the sun was setting, flushing the clay with gold, and burnishing the mould-board and the buckles on the horse. Two more furrows and the work was done. He paused for a rest, and straightened himself with difficulty. His back ached and his head throbbed, but what he saw was soothing. On the side of a hill his three sheep were haloed in gold and their long shadows sloped away from them. It was a grand sight, praise be to God, a grand sight! He bent to the plough again, his legs feeling thick and heavy. "Go on, Maggie!" he ordered. "Two more furrows and we're done."

The words whipped him to a new effort and he became light with excitement. One by one the gulls flew off and the western sky burned red. A cold breeze sharp with the smell of salt breathed in the furrows. And then he was finished; the furrows as straight as loom-threads and not a bit of ground missed. A great piece of work, thanks be to God; a great bit of work for an old man and an old mare. He put on his coat and unyoked her. She felt light and airy as he led her by the head across the cobbles. Gently he took the collar from her, the hot vapour rising into the chilled air, and with a dry sack wiped her sides and legs and neck. A great worker; none better in the whole island. He stroked her between the ears and smiled at the way she coaxingly tossed her head. He put her in the stable; later on he'd be back with a bucket of warm mash.

It was semi-dark when he turned his back on the stable and saw the orange rectangle of light in the kitchen window. It was cold, and he shivered and shrugged his shoulders as he stood listening at the door.

In the kitchen it was warm and bright. The turf was piled

high, and Martha and Kate sat on opposite sides of the hearth, Kate knitting and Martha peeling potatoes. He drew a chair to the fire and sat down between them in silence. The needles clicked rapidly, and now and then a potato plopped into the bucket. He must get out his pipe; a nice way to receive a man after a day's ploughing. The needles stopped clicking and Kate put her hands on her lap and stared at him from behind her silver-rimmed spectacles. Paddy took no notice as he went slowly on cutting his plug and grinding it between his palms. Then he spat in the fire, and Kate retorted by prodding the sods with her toe, sending sparks up the chimney. The spit hissed in the strained silence. The kettle sang and he rose to feed the mare.

"Just leave that kettle alone, Mister MacNeil," said Martha. "The mare has to be fed!"

"It's little you care about the poor dumb beast, and you out killing yourself and her, when it would suit you better to be in peeling these spuds."

"It's little you do in the house but make the few bits of meals, and it's time you were stirring yourself and getting a hard-worked man a good supper."

"If you're hard-worked, who's to blame, I ask you?" flared Kate.

He was done for now. He could always manage Martha; if he raised his voice it was the end of her. But Kate — he feared her though he wouldn't admit it to himself.

"Do you hear me, Paddy MacNeil? Who's to blame? Time and again we have told you to let the fields and have sense. But no; me bold boy must be up and leppin' about like a wild thing. And what'll the women in the island be talking about, I ask you? Ah! well we know what they'll be saying. 'It's a shame

that Paddy MacNeil's mean old sisters wouldn't hire a man to
work the land. There they have poor Paddy and his seventy
years, out in the cold of March ploughing with the old white
mare. And the three of them getting the pension. I always knew
there was a mean streak in them MacNeils.' That's what they'll
be saying, well we know it!"

"Talk sense, Kate, talk sense. Don't I know what they'll be
saying. They'll be putting me up as an example to all and
sundry. And – "

"But mark my words," interrupted Kate, shaking a needle at
him, "if you're laid up after this you can attend to your pains
yourself. I'm sick, sore and tired plastering and rubbing your
shoulder and dancing attendance on you, and God knows I'm
not able. I'm a done old woman myself, slaving from morning
to night and little thanks I get for it." Her voice quavered;
crying she'll be next. It was best to keep silent.

"Get him his supper, Martha, till we get to bed — another day
like this and I'm fit for nothing." She lifted her hands from her
lap and the needles clicked slowly, listlessly.

In silence he took his supper. He was getting tired of these
rows. When he had finished he went out with a bucket of warm
mash for the mare. He felt very weary and sleepy, but the cold
night braced him a little. The moon was up and the cobbles
shone blue-white like the scales of a salmon. Maggie stirred
when she heard the rasping handle of the bucket.

He closed the half-door of the stable, lit the candle, and sat
on an upturned tub to watch the mare feeding. It was very
still and she fed noisily, lifting her head now and again, the
bran dripping from her mouth. Above the top of the door he
could see the night-sky, the corrugated roof of the house, and
the ash tree with its bare twigs shining in the moon. A little

breeze threw its wavering pattern on the roof, and looking at it
he thought of the gulls on the clay and the cool rush of their
wings above his head. He shivered, and got up and closed the
top-half of the door. It was very still now; the mare had stopped
feeding, her tail swished gently, and the warm hay glowed in
the candlelight. There was great peace and comfort here. Under
the closed door stole the night-wind, the bits of straw around
the threshold rising gently and falling back again. A mouse
came out from under the manger, rustled towards the bucket
blinking its little eyes at the creature on the tub. Paddy squirted
a spit at it and smiled at the way it raced off. He looked at the
mare, watching slight tremors passing down her limbs. He got
up, stroked her silky neck and scratched her between the ears.
Then he gave her fresh hay and went out.

It was very peaceful with the moon shining on the fields and
the sea. He wondered if his sisters were in bed. He hesitated at
the stone-fence looking at the cold darkness of the field and the
bits of broken crockery catching the moonlight. Through the
night there came to him clear and distinct the throb, throb of a
ship's engine far out at sea. He held his breath to listen to it and
then he saw its two unsteady mastlights, rounding the headland
and moving like stars through the darkness. It made him sad to
look at it and he sighed as he turned towards the house. He
sniffed the air like a spaniel; there'd be rain before long; it
would do a world of good now that the field was ploughed.

His sisters were in bed; the lamp was lowered and the ashes
stirred. He quenched the lamp and went up to his room. The
moonlight shone in the window so he needn't bother with a
candle. He knelt on a chair to say his prayers; he'd make them
short to-night, for he was tired, very tired. But his people
couldn't be left out. The prayers came slowly. His mind wan-

dered. The golden shaft of the lighthouse swept into the room, mysteriously and quietly — light — dark — light — dark. For years he had watched that light, and years after when he'd be dead and gone it would still flash, and there'd be no son or daughter to say a prayer for him. It's a stupid thing for a man not to get married and have children to pray for him; a stupid thing indeed! It was strange to be associating death with a lighthouse in the night, but in some way that thought had come to him now that he was old, and he knew that it would always come. He didn't stop to analyse it. He got up and sat on the chair, fumbling at his coat.

He climbed into bed, the straw mattress rustling with his weight. He lay thinking of his day's work, waiting for sleep to fall upon him. He closed his eyes, but somehow sleep wouldn't come. The tiredness was wearing off him. He'd smoke for awhile, that would ease his mind. He was thinking too much; thinking kills sleep. The moonlight left the room and it became coldly dark. He stretched out his hand, groping for his pipe and matches. The effort shot a pain through his legs and he stifled a groan. At the other side of the wooden partition Kate and Martha heard him, but didn't speak. They lay listening to his movements. Then they heard the rasp of the match on the emery, heard him puffing at the pipe, and saw in their minds its warm glow in the cold darkness. There would be a long interval of silence, then the creak of his bed, and another muffled groan.

"Do you hear him?" whispered Kate. "We're going to have another time of it with him. He has himself killed. But this is the last of it!"

"He'll be harrowing the field next," said Martha.

"Harrow he will not. To-morrow, send a note to the horse-dealer in Ballycastle."

THE WHITE MARE 33

"Are you going to sell the mare, Kate?" Martha asked incredulously.

"Indeed I am. There's no sense left in that man's head while she's about."

"Will you tell Paddy?"

"I'll tell him when she's sold, and that's time enough. So off with the note first thing in the morning."

A handful of rain scattered itself on the tin roof above their heads. For awhile there was silence — deep and dark and listening. Then with a tree-like swish the rain fell, fell without ceasing, filling the room with cold streaks of noise.

Paddy lay listening to its hard pattering. He thought of the broken field soaking in the rain, and the disturbed creatures seeking shelter under the sod, rushing about with weakly legs clambering for a new home, while down in the sea the fish would be hiding in its brown tangled hair disturbed by no plough. It's strange the difference between the creatures; all the strange work of God, the God that knows all. Louder and louder fell the rain. "It's well the mare's in that night," he said to himself, "and it's well the field's ploughed." He pictured the sheep pressing into the wet rocks for shelter, and the rabbits scuttling to their holes. Then he wondered if he had closed the stable door; it was foolish to think that way; he closed it, of course he closed it. His thoughts wouldn't lie still. The crow on the thatch flew into his mind. He'd see to that villain in the morning and put a few pickles in her tail. Some day he'd have the whole house corrugated. Maybe now the kitchen'd be flooded. He was about to get up, when the rain suddenly ceased. It eased his mind, and listening now to the drip-drop of water from the eaves, he slipped into sleep.

But in the morning he didn't get up. His shoulders, arms and legs were stiff and painful. Martha brought him his breakfast, and it was a very subdued man that she saw.

"Give me a lift up, Martha, on the pillows. That's a good girl. Aisy now, aisy!" he said in a slow, pained voice.

"Do you feel bad, Paddy?"

"Bravely, Martha, bravely. There's a wee pain across me shoulder, maybe you'd give it a rub. I'll be all right now when I get a rest."

"You took too much out of yourself for one day."

"I know, I know! But it'd take any other man three days to do the same field. Listen, Martha, put the mare out on the side of the hill; a canter round will do her a world of good."

And so the first day wore on with his limbs aching, Martha coming to attend him, or Kate coming to counsel him. But from his bed he could see the mare clear as a white rock on the face of the hill, and it heartened him to watch her long tail busily swishing. On the bed beside him was his stick and on the floor a battered biscuit tin. Hour after hour he struck the tin with his stick when he wanted something — matches, tobacco, a drink, or his shoulder rubbed. And glad he was if Martha answered his knocking.

Two days passed in this way, and on the morning of the third the boat with the dealer was due. Time and again Martha went out on a hill at the back of the house, scanning the sea for the boat. At last she saw it and hurried to Kate with the news. Kate made a big bowl of warm punch and brought it to Paddy.

"How do you feel this morning?" she said when she entered the room.

"A lot aisier, thank God, a lot aisier."

"Take this now and turn in and sleep. It'll do you good."

Paddy took the warm bowl in his two hands, sipping slowly,

and giving an odd cough as the strong whisky caught his breath. Whenever he paused his eyes were on the window watching the mare on the hillside, and when he had finished, he sighed and lay back happily. His body felt deliciously warm and he smiled sweetly. Poor Kate; he misjudged her; she has a heart of corn and means well. Warm eddies of air flowed slowly through his head, stealing into every corner, filling him with a thoughtless ecstasy, and closing his eyes in sleep.

As he slept the dealer came, and the mare was sold. When he wakened he felt a queer emptiness in the room, as if something had been taken from it. Instinctively he turned to the window and looked out. The mare was nowhere to be seen and the stone-slap had been tumbled. He seized his stick and battered impatiently on the biscuit tin. He was about to get out of bed when Kate came into the room.

"The mare has got out of the field!"

"She has that and what's more she'll never set foot in it again."

He waited, waited to hear the worst, that she was sick or had broken a leg.

"The dealer was here an hour ago and I sold her, and, let me tell you, I got a good penny for her," she added a little proudly.

His anger sent a quickening flame through him, and he looked at his sister, his eyes fiercely bright and his mouth open. Catching the rail of the bed he raised himself into a sitting posture and glared at her.

"Lie down, Paddy, like a good man and quieten yourself. Sure we did it for your own good," she said, trying to make light of it, and fixing the clothes up around his chest. "What was she but a poor bit of a beast dying with age. And a good bargain we made."

"Bargain, is it? And me after rearing her since she was a wee

36   THE WHITE MARE

foal. . . . No; he'll not get her, I tell you! He'll not get her!"

"For the love of God, man, have sense, have reason!"

But he wasn't listening, he threw back the clothes and reached for his trousers. He brushed her aside with his arm, and his hands trembled as he put on his boots. He seized his stick and made for the door. They tried to stop him and he raised his stick to them. "Don't meddle with me or I'll give you a belt with this!"

He was out, taking the short-cut down by the back of the house, across the hills that led to the quay. He might be in time; they'd hardly have her in the boat yet. Stones in the gaps fell with a crash behind him and he didn't stop to build them up, not caring where sheep strayed or cattle either. His eyes were fixed on the sea, on the mainland where Maggie was going. His heart hammered wildly, hammered with sharp stinging pains, and he had to halt to ease himself.

He thought of his beast, the poor beast that hated noise and fuss, standing nervous on the pier with a rope tied round her four legs. Gradually the rope would tighten, and she would topple with a thud on the uneven stones while the boys around would cheer. It was always a sight for the young, this shipping of beasts in the little sailing boats. The thought maddened him. His breath wheezed and he licked his dry, salty lips.

And soon he came on to the road that swept in a half circle to the quay. He saw the boat and an oar sticking over the side. He wouldn't have time to go round. Below him jutted a neck of rock near which the boat would pass on her journey out. He might be able to hail them.

He splashed his way through shallow sea-pools on to the rock, scrambled over its mane of wet seaweed, until he reached the farthest point. Sweat was streaming below his hat and he

trembled weakly as he saw the black nose of the boat coming towards him. He saw the curling froth below her bow, the bending backs of the men, and heard the wooden thump of the oars. Nearer it came, gathering speed. A large wave tilted the boat and he saw the white side of his mare, lying motionless between the beams. They were opposite him now, a hundred yards from him. He raised his stick and called, but he seemed to have lost his voice. He waved and called again, his voice sounding strange and weak. The man in the stern waved back as he would to a child. The boat passed the rock, leaving a wedge of calm water in her wake. The noise of the oars stopped and the sail filled in the breeze. For a long time he looked at the receding boat, his spirit draining from him. A wave washed up the rock, frothing at his feet, and he turned wearily away, going slowly back the road that led home.

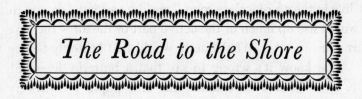

The Road to the Shore

" 'TIS going to be a lovely day, thanks be to God," sighed Sister Paul to herself, as she rubbed her wrinkled hands together and looked out at the thrushes hopping across the lawn. "And it was a lovely day last year and the year before," she mused, and in her mind saw the fresh face of the sea where, in an hour or two, she and the rest of the community would be enjoying their annual trip to the shore. "And God knows it may be my last trip," she said resignedly, and gazed abstractedly at a butterfly that was purring its wings against the sunny pane. She opened the window and watched the butterfly swing out into the sweet air, zig-zagging down to a cushion of flowers that bordered the lawn. "Isn't it well Sister Clare wasn't here," she said to herself, "for she'd be pestering the very soul out of me with her questions about butterflies and birds and flowers and the fall of dew." She gave her girdle of beads a slight rattle. Wasn't it lovely to think of the pleasure that little butterfly would have when it found the free air under its wings again and its little feet pressing on the soft petals of the flowers and not on the hard pane. She always maintained it was better to enjoy Nature without searching and probing and chattering about the what and the where and the wherefore. But Sister Clare! — what she got out of it all, goodness only knew, for she'd give nobody a minute's peace — not a moment's peace would

she give to a saint, living or dead. "How long would that butterfly live in the air of a class-room," she'd be asking; "do you think
it would use up much of the active part of the air — the oxygen
part, I mean. . . . What family would that butterfly belong to
. . . You know it's wrong to say that a butterfly lives only a
day. . . . When I am teaching my little pupils I always try to
be accurate. I don't believe in stuffing their heads with fantasti-
cal nonsense however pleasurable it may be . . ." Sister Paul
turned round as if someone had suddenly walked into the room,
and she was relieved when she saw nothing only the quiet
vacancy of the room, the varnished desks with the sun on them
and their reflections on the parquet floor.

She hoped she wouldn't be sitting beside Clare in the car
to-day! She'd have no peace with her — not a bit of peace to
look out at the countryside and see what changes had taken
place inside twelve months. But Reverend Mother, she knew,
would arrange all that — and if it'd be her misfortune to be
parked beside Clare she'd have to accept it with resignation;
yes, with resignation, and in that case her journey to the sea
would be like a pilgrimage.

At that moment a large limousine drove up the gravel path,
and as it swung round to the convent door she saw the flowers
flow across its polished sides in a blur of colour. She hurried out
of the room and down the stairs. In the hall Sister Clare and
Sister Benignus were standing beside two baskets and Reverend
Mother was staring at the stairs. "Where were you, Sister Paul?"
she said with mild reproof. "We searched the whole building for
you. . . . We're all ready this ages. . . . And Sister Francis
has gone to put out the cat. Do you remember last year it had
been in all the time we were at the shore and it ate the bacon."
As she spoke a door closed at the end of the corridor and Sister

Francis came along, polishing her specs with the corner of her veil. Reverend Mother glanced away from her, that continual polishing of the spectacles irritated her; and then that empty expression on Sister Francis' face when the spectacles were off — vacuous that's what it was!

"All ready now," Reverend Mother tried to say without any trace of perturbation. Sister Clare and Sister Benignus lifted two baskets at their feet, Reverend Mother opened the hall-door, and they all glided out into the flat sunlight.

The doors of the car were wide open, the engine purring gently, and a perfume of new leather fingering the air. The chauffeur, a young man, touched his cap and stood deferentially to the side. Reverend Mother surveyed him quickly, noting his clean-bright face and white collar. "I think there'll be room for us all in the back," she said.

"There's a seat in the front, Sister," the young man said, touching his cap again.

"Just put the baskets on it, if you please," said Reverend Mother. And Sister Clare who, at that moment, was smiling at her own grotesque reflection in the back of the car came forward with her basket, Sister Benignus following. Sister Paul sighed audibly and fingered her girdle of beads.

"Now, Sister Paul, you take one of the corner seats, Sister Clare you sit beside her, and Sister Benignus and Sister Francis on the spring-up seats facing them — they were just made for you, the tiny tots!" And they all laughed, a brittle laugh that emphasised the loveliness of the day.

When they were all seated, Reverend Mother made sure that the hall-door was locked, glanced at the fastened windows, and then stood for a minute watching the gardener who was pushing his lawn-mower with unusual vigour and concentration. He stopped abruptly when her shadow fell across his path. "And, Jack," she said, as if continuing a conversation that had been interrupted, "You'll have that lawn finished to-day?"

"Yes, Mother," and he took off his hat and held it in front of his breast. "To be sure I'll have it finished to-day. Sure what'd prevent me to finish it, and this the grandest day God sent this many a long month — a wholesome day!"

"And, Jack, I noticed some pebbles on the lawn yesterday — white ones."

"I remarked them myself, Mother. A strange terrier disporting himself in the garden done it."

"Did it!"

"Yes, Mother, he did it with his two front paws, scratching at the edge of the lawn like it was a rabbit burrow. He done it yesterday, and when I clodded him off the grounds he'd the impertinence to go out a different way than he came in. But I've now his entrances and exits all blocked and barricaded and I'm afraid he'll have to find some other constituency to disport himself. Dogs is a holy terror for bad habits."

"Be sure and finish it all to-day," she said with some impatience. She turned to go away, hesitated, and turned back. "By the way, Jack, if there are any drips of oil made by the car on the gravel you'll scuffle fresh pebbles over them."

"I'll do that. But you need have no fear of oil from her engine," and he glanced over at the limousine, "she'll be as clean as a Swiss clock. 'Tis them grocery vans that leak — top, tail and middle."

Crossing to the car, she heard with a feeling of pleasure the surge of the lawn-mover over the grass. Presently the car swung out of the gate on to a tree-lined road at the edge of the town. The nuns relaxed, settled themselves more comfortably in their seats and chatted about the groups on bicycles that were all heading for the shore.

"We will go to the same quiet strip as last year," said Reverend Mother, and then as she glanced out of the window a villa on top of a hill drew her attention. "There's a house that has been built since last year," she said.

"No, no," said Sister Francis. "It's more than a year old for I remember seeing it last year," and she peered at it through her spectacles.

Reverend Mother spoke through the speaking-tube to the driver: "Is that villa on the hill newly built?" she asked.

He stopped the car. "A doctor by the name of McGrath built it two years ago," he said. "He's married to a daughter of Solicitor O' Kane."

"Oh, thank you," said Reverend Mother; and the car proceeded slowly up the long hill above the town.

Sister Francis took off her spectacles, blew her breath on them, and rubbed them with her handkerchief. She took another look at the villa and said with obvious pride: "A fine site, indeed. I remember last year that they had that little gadget over the door."

"The architrave," said Sister Clare importantly.

"Aye," said Sister Paul, and she looked out at the trees and below them the black river with its strings of froth moving through the valley. How lovely it would be, she thought, to sit on the edge of that river, dabble her parched feet in it and send bubbles out into the race of the current. She had often done that when she was a child, and now that river and its trees, which she only saw once in a year, brought her childhood back to her. She sighed and opened the window so as to hear the mumble of the river far below them. The breeze whorled in, and as it lifted their veils they all smiled, invigorated by the fresh loveliness of the air. A bumble bee flew in and crawled up the pane at Reverend Mother's side of the car. She opened the window and assisted the bee towards the opening with the tip of her fountain-pen, but the bee clung to the pen and as she tried to shake it free the wind carried it in again. "Like everything else it hates to leave you," said Sister Benignus. Reverend Mother smiled and the bee flew up to the roof of the car and then alighted on the window beside Sister Paul. Sister Paul swept the bee to safety with the back of her hand.

"You weren't one bit afraid of it," said Sister Clare. "And if it had stung you, you would in a way have been responsible for its death. If it had been a Queen bee — though Queens wouldn't be flying at this time of the year — you would have been responsible for the deaths of potential thousands. A Queen bumble bee lays over two thousand eggs in one season!"

" 'Tis a great pity we haven't a hen like that," put in Sister Francis, and they all laughed except Sister Clare. Sister Francis laughed till her eyes watered and, once more, she took off her spectacles. Reverend Mother fidgeted slightly and, in order to control her annoyance, she fixed her gaze on Sister Clare and asked her to continue her interesting account of the life of bumble bees. Sister Paul put her hands in her sleeves and sought distraction in the combings of cloud that streaked the sky.

Reverend Mother pressed her toe on the floor of the car end, instead of listening to Sister Clare, she was glaring unconsciously at Sister Francis who was tapping her spectacles on the palm of her hand and giving an odd laugh.

"Your spectacles are giving you much trouble to-day," she broke in, unable any longer to restrain herself. "Perhaps you would like to sit in the middle. It may provide your poor eyes with some rest."

"No, thank you," said Sister Francis, "I like watching the crowds of cyclists passing on the road. But sometimes the sun glints on their handlebars and blinds me for a moment and makes me feel that a tiny thread or two has congregated on my lenses. It's my imagination of course."

"Maybe you would care to have a look at *St. Anthony's Annals,*" and Reverend Mother handed her the magazine.

"Thank you, Mother. I'll keep it until we reach the shore, for the doctor told me not to read in moving vehicles."

The car rolled on slowly and when it reached the top of a hill, where there was a long descent of five miles to the sea, a strange silence came over the nuns, and each became absorbed in her own premeditation on the advancing day. "Go slowly down the hill," Reverend Mother ordered the driver.

Boys sailed past them on bicycles; when some did so with their hands off the handlebars a little cry of amazement would break from Sister Francis and she would discuss with Sister Clare the reckless irresponsibility of boys and the worry they must bring to their parents.

Suddenly at a bend on the hill they all looked at Sister Paul for she was excitedly drawing their attention to a line of young poplars. "Look, look!" she was saying, "look at the way their leaves are dancing and not a flicker out of the other trees. And to think I never noticed them before!"

"I think they are aspens," said Sister Clare, "and anyway they are not indigenous to this country."

"We had four poplars in our garden when I was growing up — black poplars, my father called them," said Sister Paul, lost in her own memory.

"What family did they belong to? There's *angustifolia, lauri-folia,* and *balsamifera* and others among the poplar family."

"I don't know what family they belonged to," Sister Paul went on quietly. "I only know they were beautiful — beautiful in very early spring when every tree and twig around them would still be bleak — and there they were bursting into leaf, a brilliant yellow leaf like a flake of sunshine. My father, God be good to his kindly soul, planted four of them when I was young, for there were four in our family, all girls, and one of the trees my father called Kathleen, another Teresa, another Eileen, and lastly my own, Maura. And I remember how he used to stand at the dining-room window gazing out at the young poplars with the frost white and hard around them. 'I see a leaf or two coming on Maura,' he used to say, and we would all rush to the window and gaze into the garden, each of us fastening her eye on her own tree and then measuring its growth of leaf with the others. And to the one whose tree was first in leaf he used to give a book or a pair of rosary beads. . . . Poor Father," she sighed, and fumbled in her sleeve for her handkerchief.

"Can you not think of what special name those trees had?" pressed Clare. "Did their leaves tremble furiously — *tremula, tremuloides.*"

"They didn't quiver very much, " said Sister Paul, her head bowed. "My father didn't plant aspens, I remember. He told us it was from an aspen that Our Saviour's rood was made, and because their leaves remember the Crucifixion they are always trembling. . . . But our poplars had a lovely warm perfume when they were leafing and that perfume always reminded my father of autumn. Wasn't that strange?" she addressed the whole car, "a tree coming into leaf and it reminding my poor father of autumn."

"I know its family now," said Clare, clapping her hands together. "*Balsamifera* — that's the family it belonged to — it's a native of Northern Italy."

"And I remember," said Paul, folding and unfolding her handkerchief on her lap, "how my poor father had no gum once to wrap up a newspaper that he was posting. It was in winter and he went out to the poplars and dabbed his finger here and there on the sticky buds and smeared it on the edge of the wrapping paper."

"That was enough to kill the buds," said Clare. "The gum, as you call it, is their only protective against frost."

"It was himself he killed," said Paul. "He had gone out from a warm fire in his slippers, out into the bleak air and got his death."

"And what happened to the poplars?" said Clare. But Sister Paul had turned her head to the window again and was trying to stifle the tears that were rising to her eyes.

"What other trees grew in your neighbourhood?" continued Clare. Sister Paul didn't seem to hear her, but when the question was repeated she turned and said slowly: "I'm sorry that I don't know their names. But my father, Lord have mercy on him, used to say that a bird could leap from branch to branch for ten miles around without using its wings."

Sister Clare smiled and Reverend Mother nudged her with her elbow, signing to her to keep quiet; and when she, herself, glanced at Paul she saw the sun shining through the fabric of her veil and a handkerchief held furtively to her eyes.

There was silence now in the sun-filled car while outside cyclists continued to pass them, free-wheeling down the long hill. Presently there was a rustle of paper in the car as Sister Francis drew forth from her deep pocket a bag of soft peppermints, stuck together by the heat. Carefully she peeled the bits of paper off the sweets, and as she held out the bag to Reverend Mother she said: "Excuse my fingers." But Reverend Mother shook her head, and Clare and Benignus, seeing that she had refused, felt it would be improper for them to accept. Francis shook the bag towards Paul but since she had her eyes closed, as if in prayer, she neither saw nor heard what was being offered to her. *"In somno pacis,"* said Francis, popping two peppermints into her own mouth and hiding the bag in her wide sleeve. "A peppermint is soothing and cool on a hot day like this," she added with apologetic good-nature.

A hot smell of peppermint drifted around the car. Reverend Mother lowered her window to its full length, and though the air rushed in in soft folds around her face it was unable to quench the flaming odour. Somehow, for Reverend Mother, the day, that had hardly begun yet, was spoiled by an old nun with foolish habits and by a young nun unwise enough not to know when to stop questioning. Everything was going wrong, and it would not surprise her that before evening clouds of rain would blow in from the sea and blot out completely the soft loveliness of the sunny day. Once more she looked at Paul, and, seeing her head bowed in thought, she knew that there was some aspect of the countryside, some shape in cloud or bush, that brought back to Paul a sweet but sombre childhood. For herself she had no such memories — there was nothing in her own life, she thought, only a mechanical ordering, a following of routine, that may have brought some pleasure into other peoples' lives but none to her own. However, she'd do her best to make the day pleasant for them; after all, it was only one day in the year and if the eating of peppermints gave Sister Francis some satisfaction it was not right to thwart her.

She smiled sweetly then at Francis, and as Francis offered the sweets once more, and she was stretching forward to take one there was a sudden dunt to the back of the car and a crash of something falling on the road. The car stopped and the nuns looked at one another, their heads bobbing in consternation. They saw the driver raise himself slowly from his seat, walk back the road, and return again with a touch of his cap at the window.

"A slight accident, Sister," he said, addressing Reverend Mother. "A cyclist crashed into our back wheel. But it's nothing serious, I think."

Reverend Mother went out leaving the door open, and through it there came the free sunlight, the cool air, and the hum of people talking. She was back again in a few minutes with her handkerchief dabbed with blood, and collected other handkerchiefs from the nuns, who followed her out on to the road. Sister Paul stood back and saw amongst the bunch of people a young man reclining on the bank of the road, a hand to his head. "I can't stand the sight of blood," she said to herself, her fingers clutching her rosary beads. She beckoned to a lad who was resting on his bicycle: "Is he badly hurt, lad? He'll not die, will he?"

"Not a bit of him, Sister. He had his coat folded over the handlebars and the sleeve of it caught in the wheel and flung him against the car."

"Go up, like a decent boy, and have a good look at him again."

But before the lad had reached the group the chauffeur had assisted the injured man to his feet and was leading him to the car. The handkerchiefs were tied like a turban about his head, his trousers were torn at the knee, and a holy medal was pinned to his braces.

"Put his coat on or he'll catch cold," Reverend Mother was saying.

"Och, Sister, don't worry about me," the man was saying. "Sure it was my own fault. Ye weren't to blame at all. I'll go back again on my own bicycle — I'm fit enough."

Reverend Mother consulted the chauffeur and whatever advice he gave her the injured man was put into the back of the car. Sister Francis was ordered into the vacant seat beside the driver, the baskets were handed to Paul and Clare, and when the man's bicycle was tied to the crate they drove off for the hospital in the town.

The young man, sitting between Reverend Mother and Sister Paul, shut his eyes in embarrassment, and when the blood oozed through the pile of handkerchiefs Reverend Mother took the serviettes from the baskets and tied them round his head and under his chin, and all the time the man kept repeating: "I'm a sore trouble to you, indeed. And sure it was my own fault." She told him to button his coat or he would catch cold, and when he had done so she noticed a Total Abstinence badge in the lapel.

"A good clean-living man," she thought, and to think that he was the one to meet with an injury while many an old drunkard could travel the roads of Ireland on a bicycle and arrive home without pain or scratch or cough.

"'Tis a blessing of God you weren't killed," she said, with a rush of protectiveness, and she reached for the thermos flask from the basket and handed the man a cup of tea.

Now and again Sister Paul would steal a glance at him, but the sight of his pale face and the cup trembling in his hand and rattling on the saucer made her turn to the window where she tried to lose herself in contemplation. But all her previous mood was now scattered from her mind, and she could think of nothing only the greatness of Reverend Mother and the cool way she took command of an incident that would have left the rest of them weak and confused.

"How are you feeling now?" she could hear Reverend Mother asking. "Would you like another sandwich?"

"No, thank you, Sister, sure I had my good breakfast in me before I left the house. I'm a labouring man and since I'm out of work this past three months my wife told me to go off on the bike and have a swim with myself. I was going to take one of the youngsters on the bar of the bike but my wife wouldn't let me."

"She had God's grace about her," said Reverend Mother. "That should be a lesson to you," and as she refilled his cup from the thermos flask she thought that if the young man had been killed they, in a way, would have had to provide his widow and children with some help. "And we were only travelling slowly," she found herself saying aloud.

"Sure, Sister, no one knows that better than myself. You were keeping well in to your own side of the road and when I was ready to sail past you on the hill my coat caught in the front wheel and my head hit the back of your car."

"S-s-s," and the nuns drew in their breath with shrinking solicitude.

The car drove up to the hospital, and after Reverend Mother had consulted the doctor and was told that the wound was only a slight abrasion and contusion she returned light-heartedly to the car. Sister Clare made no remark when she heard the news but as the wheels of the car rose and fell on the road they seemed to echo what was in her mind: *abrasion and contusion, abrasion and contusion.* "Abrasion and contusion of what?" she asked herself. "Surely the doctor wouldn't say 'head' — abrasion and contusion of the head?" No, there must be some medical term that Reverend Mother had witheld from them, and as she was about to probe Reverend Mother for the answer the car swung unexpectedly into the convent avenue. "Oh," she said with disappointment, and when alighting from the car and seeing Sister Francis give the remains of her sweets to the chauffeur she knew that for her, too, the day was at an end.

They all passed inside except Reverend Mother who stood on the steps at the door noting the quiet silence of the grounds and the heat-shadows flickering above the flower-beds. With a mocking smile she saw the lawn-mower at rest on the uncut lawn and found herself mimicking the gardener: "I'll have it all finished to-day, Sister, I'll have it all finished to-day." She put a hand to her throbbing head and crossed the gravel path to look for him, and there in the clump of laurel bushes she found him fast asleep, his hat over his face to keep off the flies, and three empty porter bottles beside him. She tiptoed away from him. "He has had a better day than we have had," she said to herself, "so let him sleep it out, for it's the last he'll have at my expense . . . Oh, drink is a curse;" and she thought of the injury that had befallen the young man with the Abstinence Badge and he as sober as any judge. Then she drew up suddenly as something quick and urgent came into her mind: "Of course! — he would take the job as gardener, and he unemployed this past three months!" With head erect she sped quickly across the grass and into the convent. Sister Paul was still in the corridor when she saw Reverend Mother lift the phone and ring up the hospital: "Is he still there . . . He's all right . . . that's good . . . Would you tell him to call to see me sometime this afternoon." There was a transfigured look on her face as she put down the receiver and strode across to Sister Paul. "Sister Paul," she said, "you may tell the other Sisters that to-morrow we will set out again for the shore." Sister Paul smiled and whisked away down the corridor: "Isn't Reverend Mother great the way she can handle things," she said to herself, "and to think that on to-morrow I'll be able to see the poplars again."

The Wild Duck's Nest

THE sun was setting, spilling gold light on the low western hills of Rathlin Island. A small boy walked jauntily along a hoof-printed path that wriggled between the folds of these hills and opened out into a crater-like valley on the cliff-top. Presently he stopped as if remembering something, then suddenly he left the path, and began running up one of the hills. When he reached the top he was out of breath and stood watching streaks of light radiating from golden-edged clouds, the scene reminding him of a picture he had seen of the Transfiguration. A short distance below him was the cow standing at the edge of a reedy lake. Colm ran down to meet her waving his stick in the air, and the wind rumbling in his ears made him give an exultant whoop which splashed upon the hills in a shower of echoed sound. A flock of gulls lying on the short grass near the lake rose up languidly, drifting like blown snowflakes over the rim of the cliff.

The lake faced west and was fed by a stream, the drainings of the semi-circling hills. One side was open to the winds from the sea and in winter a little outlet trickled over the cliffs making a black vein in their grey sides. The boy lifted stones and began throwing them into the lake, weaving web after web on its calm surface. Then he skimmed the water with flat stones, some of them jumping the surface and coming to rest on the other side.

He was delighted with himself and after listening to his echoing
shouts of delight he ran to fetch his cow. Gently he tapped her
on the side and reluctantly she went towards the brown-mudded
path that led out of the valley. The boy was about to throw a
final stone into the lake when a bird flew low over his head, its
neck a-strain, and its orange-coloured legs clear in the soft light.
It was a wild duck. It circled the lake twice, thrice, coming
lower each time and then with a nervous flapping of wings it
skidded along the surface, its legs breaking the water into a
series of silvery arcs. Its wings closed, it lit silently, gave a slight
shiver, and began pecking indifferently at the water.

Colm with dilated eyes eagerly watched it making for the
farther end of the lake. It meandered between tall bulrushes,
its body, black and solid as stone against the greying water.
Then as if it had sunk it was gone. The boy ran stealthily along
the bank looking away from the lake, pretending indifference.
When he came opposite to where he had last seen the bird he
stopped and peered through the sighing reeds whose shadows
streaked the water in a maze of black strokes. In front of him
was a soddy islet guarded by the spears of sedge and separated
from the bank by a narrow channel of water. The water wasn't
too deep — he could wade across with care.

Rolling up his short trousers he began to wade, his arms out-
stretched, and his legs brown and stunted in the mountain
water. As he drew near the islet, his feet sank in the cold mud
and bubbles winked up at him. He went more carefully and
nervously. Then one trouser fell and dipped into the water; the
boy dropped his hands to roll it up, he unbalanced, made a
splashing sound, and the bird arose with a squawk and whirred
away over the cliffs. For a moment the boy stood frightened.
Then he clambered on to the wet-soaked sod of land, which

was spattered with sea gulls' feathers and bits of wind-blown rushes.

Into each hummock he looked, pulling back the long grass. At last he came on the nest, facing seawards. Two flat rocks dimpled the face of the water and between them was a neck of land matted with coarse grass containing the nest. It was untidily built of dried rushes, straw and feathers, and in it lay one solitary egg. Colm was delighted. He looked around and saw no one. The nest was his. He lifted the egg, smooth and green as the sky, with a faint tinge of yellow like the reflected light from a buttercup; and then he felt he had done wrong. He put it back. He knew he shouldn't have touched it and he wondered would the bird forsake the nest. A vague sadness stole over him and he felt in his heart he had sinned. Carefully smoothing out his footprints he hurriedly left the islet and ran after his cow. The sun had now set and the cold shiver of evening enveloped him, chilling his body and saddening his mind.

In the morning he was up and away to school. He took the grass rut that edged the road for it was softer on the bare feet. His house was the last on the western headland and after a mile or so he was joined by Paddy McFall; both boys dressed in similar hand-knitted blue jerseys and grey trousers carried home-made school bags. Colm was full of the nest and as soon as he joined his companion he said eagerly: "Paddy, I've a nest — a wild duck's with one egg."

"And how do you know it's a wild duck's?" asked Paddy slightly jealous.

"Sure I saw her with my own two eyes, her brown speckled back with a crow's patch on it, and her yellow legs ——"

"Where is it?" interrupted Paddy in a challenging tone.

"I'm not going to tell you, for you'd rob it!"

"Aach! I suppose it's a tame duck's you have or maybe an old gull's."

Colm put out his tongue at him. "A lot you know!" he said, "for a gull's egg has spots and this one is greenish-white, for I had it in my hand."

And then the words he didn't want to hear rushed from Paddy in a mocking chant, "You had it in your hand! . . . She'll forsake it! She'll forsake it! She'll forsake it!" he said, skipping along the road before him.

Colm felt as if he would choke or cry with vexation.

His mind told him that Paddy was right, but somehow he couldn't give in to it and he replied: "She'll not forsake it! She'll not! I know she'll not!"

But in school his faith wavered. Through the windows he could see moving sheets of rain — rain that dribbled down the panes filling his mind with thoughts of the lake creased and chilled by wind; the nest sodden and black with wetness; and the egg cold as a cave stone. He shivered from the thoughts and fidgeted with the inkwell cover, sliding it backwards and forwards mechanically. The mischievous look had gone from his eyes and the school day dragged on interminably. But at last they were out in the rain, Colm rushing home as fast as he could.

He was no time at all at his dinner of potatoes and salted fish until he was out in the valley now smoky with drifts of slanting rain. Opposite the islet he entered the water. The wind was blowing into his face, rustling noisily the rushes heavy with the dust of rain. A moss-cheeper, swaying on a reed like a mouse, filled the air with light cries of loneliness.

The boy reached the islet, his heart thumping with excitement, wondering did the bird forsake. He went slowly, quietly, on to the strip of land that led to the nest. He rose on his toes,

looking over the ledge to see if he could see her. And then every muscle tautened. She was on, her shoulders hunched up, and her bill lying on her breast as if she were asleep. Colm's heart hammered wildly in his ears. She hadn't forsaken. He was about to turn stealthily away. Something happened. The bird moved, her neck straightened, twitching nervously from side to side. The boy's head swam with lightness. He stood transfixed. The wild duck with a panicky flapping, rose heavily, and flew off towards the sea. . . . A guilty silence enveloped the boy. . . . He turned to go away, hesitated, and glanced back at the bare nest; it'd be no harm to have a look. Timidly he approached it, standing straight, and gazing over the edge. There in the nest lay two eggs. He drew in his breath with delight, splashed quickly from the island, and ran off whistling in the rain.

Aunt Suzanne

THE McKinleys all went down to the station to meet their Aunt Suzanne, who was coming to take care of them now that their mother was dead. Mary, the eldest, was fifteen; Annie was eleven; and wee Arthur was nine. They boarded a tram at the foot of the street, and after much pleading and hauling, Arthur got them to go up on top. He loved the top of the tram, to kneel on the ribbed seat, and to feel the wind dunting his face or combing his hair.

To-day he leaned over the iron railings looking down at the top of the driver's cap: the cap was shiny and greasy, and a large lump knuckled up in the centre. Arthur tried to light a spit on it when Mary wasn't looking, but at last she spied him, slapped his hands, promising that never again would she come on top with him. The kneeling on the seat had imprinted red furrows on his knees, and he fingered them till a sandwich-man caught his eye. He stood up, staring at the walking triangle of boards, watching the legs of the man and wondering how he could see out. When he asked Mary how the man could see, Annie chimed in: "You're a stupid fella! Did you not see the peep-hole in the board?" Arthur made up his mind there and then that he would be a sandwich-man travelling round and round the streets, just like a motor-car.

At the station they had to wait, Mary telling and retelling

Arthur not to be forgetting his manners, occasionally taking his hands out of his pockets, and pulling down his jersey. Overhead arched the glass roof, pigeons cooing along the girders and sparrows chirping in and out. Three taxi drivers sat on the running-board of a motor reading a newspaper, and near them a cab horse fed wheezily out of a nosebag. There was plenty of time, and Mary put a penny in a chocolate machine, letting Arthur pull out the drawer. The chocolate was neatly wrapped in silver paper, but when she went to divide it, it was so thin that it crumbled in her hands.

As Arthur ate his chcolate he was fascinated by a huge advertisement — a smiling girl poised on a white-rigged bottle that splashed through the sea. He could read some of the words, and Annie helped him to read others, but when he asked unanswerable questions about the bottle, Annie told him to look out for the train and play at who-would-see-it-first coming in along the shiny lines.

A bell began to ring somewhere, and the taxi drivers got up, dusting their clothes. Mary moved along the platform, the steel bumpers and the noisy trucks of the porters filling Arthur's mind with terrifying wonder. Presently there came a thundering rumble and the train came panting in, smoke hitting the glass roof with all its might.

Mary fidgeted: "Now you two, hold on to me tight. Don't get lost! Look out for Aunt Suzanne! She's small; she'll be in black! She has a . . . She has a . . . She has a . . . Oh, I see her! There she is!" People hurried past, brushing roughly against wee Arthur till he was ready to cry from fright, but Mary's gleeful shouts sent a breathless weak excitement over him. And then, as if she had jumped out of the ground, he was looking up at Aunt Suzanne.

She was a small woman, not as tall as Mary, with a black plush coat, a yellow crinkly face, and a black hat skewered with enormous hat-pins. But as he looked down below her coat, he saw something funny: he saw one boot, and where the other should have been was a ring of iron. Mary nipped him: "Aunt Suzanne's speaking to you."

"And who's this?"

"That's Arthur."

"A lovely little boy. God bless him," she said, touching his cheek with a cold hand.

"And what book are you in?" she added.

"Third," Mary replied for him.

"Third! Well, now, isn't that a great little man! . . . And this is Annie. Well, well, she was only a wee baby when I saw her last — a lovely, wee baby. Tut, tut, tut, how the time flies!"

Annie relieved her of a band-box; Mary took her black, glossy bag, and linking her by the arm they began to move off along the platform. Occasionally Aunt Suzanne would stop and say: "Well, well, it's just like old times again!" But the clink of the iron foot on the pavement made Arthur twist and turn so that he could see how it moved. When Mary saw him gaping she scowled at him, and for the moment he would look in front, fixing his gaze on a horse or a tram, but always there came the clink-clink of iron on stone, and always he would turn his head and stare at the foot, then the iron, the boot again, and then the . . .

"Walk on a minute, Auntie. Arthur's boot's loosed," and Mary pushed Arthur to the side and began to untie his laces and bow them tightly again, until Aunt Suzanne and Annie were out of hearing. "Now!" she said, pointing a threatening finger at him. "If I-get-you-looking at Auntie's leg, there's no telling what I'll give you. Do you hear me? Come along and be a good boy. You'll never get out with us again! Never!" She tightened up his tie and pulled him along by the hand.

Into a tram they got, Annie and Arthur sitting opposite Mary and Aunt Suzanne.

"No, no, child, dear, I'll get them," said Aunt Suzanne when the conductor came along. Mary handed the tickets to Arthur, but he only turned them over in his hand, and then his eyes swivelled to the iron foot that didn't reach the floor. And then he looked up at his Auntie's face and stared at it fixedly. Below her hat were two wings of grey hair, and from the corners of her buttony nose were two deep lines, making a letter A with her mouth. There were a few white hairs on her chin, and her eyes were brown and sunken. Suddenly the eyes narrowed, and Arthur returned his Auntie's smile. He decided that he was going to like her, but he hoped he hadn't to sleep with her because of her iron leg.

Passing up the street he felt that all the wee lads would be gazing at his Auntie with her clop-clink, clink-clop. If she'd only cover it with a stocking and put pasteboard inside it, nobody'd hear it or know what it was. Suddenly he left them and ran over to three of his companions who were standing with their hands behind their backs looking at a baker's horse. To show off before his Auntie he ran under the horse's legs and out by the other side.

"Holy misfortunes, what a child!" said Auntie Sue, frightened to a standstill.

"Arthur!" yelled Mary.

Arthur came running back and Mary gave him a stinging smack on the jaw. "You've been working for that this day!"

All the way to the house and into the house, he sobbed and

sniffed: "Wait'll me Da comes home till ye see what ye'll get!"

"That's just it," said Mary. "Me father has him spoilt!"

"Sh-sh-sh, big little mans don't cry. Tut-tut," pleaded Auntie Sue. "Give me my bag till you see what I have for you — and none for the rest," she added, casting a wink at Mary and Annie. When Arthur heard the happy rustle of paper, his sobs became less frequent, and when he received a piece of sugar-stick coloured like a barber's pole he sat on the fender sucking contentedly, and even suffered Mary to wipe his face with a damp cloth.

Aunt Suzanne rested on the sofa looking with admiration at the clean tiles of the floor, the white-scrubbed table, and at the mantelpiece where two delph dogs guarded a row of shining brassware: horseshoes, two candlesticks, a rigged ship, and a three-legged pot containing a bunch of matches. "Yiv the place shining," she said proudly. "Did you do it all by yourself, Mary? . . . You and Annie. Och, och, but it's nice to see two sisters agreeable."

Mary took the band-box and the glossy bag and put them in a room off the kitchen, and while she poked the fire to hurry on the kettle, Annie spread a clean newspaper on the table and laid down the cups and saucers; Aunt Suzanne stretched herself out on the sofa, and wee Arthur was sent out to play till the big people had finished their tea.

From the table they could see, through the curtain on the window, the red-bricked houses on the opposite side of the street; and many a question Mary had to answer about the neighbours — the gossipy ones, the friendly ones, and the borrowing ones.

Just when they had finished their tea, Arthur came crying into the yard and battered impatiently at the scullery door.

"What's up now?" said Mary, letting him in. He didn't answer, but ran to Auntie Sue. She took him in her arms and nursed him, but he scratched his cheek on a brooch in her breast and cried all the more.

"What's wrong, my pigeon? What's wrong, my darling? Tell your Auntie Sue."

"The wee lads called you iron-hoof and cork leg," he whimpered.

"There's a cheeky lot of gets about this place," said Mary. "Wait'll I get my hands on some of them."

"And what did you say to them?" Auntie asked, shaking him to and fro.

"I said you hadn't a cork leg," he replied, bursting into more tears.

"There, there!" consoled Auntie.

"Maybe God'll give some of them a bad leg before very long," put in Annie.

"God forbid, child dear; sure, they're only childer and mean no harm."

They were relieved when Arthur stopped whimpering, for they never knew at what time their father would step in on them and find wee Arthur in tears. It was late that night, however, when he came home from work in the flour mill, and they had all gone to bed except Auntie Sue.

Whilst he shaved in a looking-glass hung to a nail in the mantelpiece, his face under the gaslight, he kept up a chat with her. Later, he talked about old times and about Armagh, where Susie came from; then he fell silent, looking at the flames nodding and leaping in the fire and the flakes of soot shivering in the wide chimney. She, too, fell silent with her hands joined on her lap, looking at the wrinkles of flour in his boots, and thinking of his poor wife, her own sister. And then, without preface, he turned to her: "Tell me, Susie, are you off the bottle?"

"Off the bottle!" she started. "Not a drop of strong drink has wet my lips this many a long year. I forget the taste of it — that's the God's truth, Daniel."

"I'm glad to hear that. It's the divil's own poison. Poor Katy, God be good to her, would be here now only for it."

"Aye, aye," she sighed, taking a handerkerchief and dabbing her eyes.

He looked at her awkwardly for a minute and said: "You'll be dead tired after your journey. . . Be good to the childer, Susie, and keep a tight eye on wee Arthur. . . Good night, now!"

After the first week or two Arthur and Auntie became great friends. He no longer stared at her iron-leg, and no longer paid heed to its stamping up the stairs or its clinking across the tiles. Auntie Sue was good to him and paid him halfpennies for gathering cinders. With a battered bucket, a piece of cardboard covering the hole in the bottom, he would go out to the waste ground at the back of the small houses. There the neighbours flung out their ashes, cabbage stalks, and potato-skins. He would squat for hours on his hunkers, rummaging with a stick for the blue cinders, until the bucket would be nearly filled. Then up with him carrying the bucket in front with his two arms under the handle. Aunt Suzanne would open the yard door at his knock. "That's the man! Them'll make a grand fire. There's nothing like cinders," and out would come the black purse, and a penny or a halfpenny would be squeezed into an eager hand.

Then, one warm day, when Annie and Mary were down the town, Arthur wanted to earn a penny for the pictures, and, as usual, he took out the bucket to gather cinders. The cinders were hot under the sun, and near him bare-footed boys sat with pieces of mirror glass, reflecting the sunlight into the cool corners of the houses. Men, waistcoats unbuttoned, sat with newspapers over their heads, and on the yard walls thrushes in their cages sang madly in the sun. Dogs lounged about with hanging tongues and heaving sides. But Arthur worked on.

The sun scorched down on him and a creak came in his neck, but only a few cinders lay in the bottom of the bucket. He sighed, wiped the sweat from his face with the sleeve of his jersey, and hoked on.

He felt thirsty and came into the yard where the tiles burned under his bare feet. All the doors were open, but the air was still. Two fly-papers covered with flies hung from the clothes-line in the kitchen. He padded around for Aunt Suzanne and pushed open her room door; and there she was sitting on the bed with a black bottle to her mouth.

"Aw, give's a slug?"

"Merciful God, where did you come from? You put the heart out of me!" She twisted the cork into the bottle and slapped it tight with the heel of her hand. "Pwt-th-t!" she said in disgust, making a wry face. "Rotten medicine! Worse than castor, but poor Auntie has to take it."

She went to the sink in the scullery, the splashing tap spilling coolness into the air. Arthur held the wet cup in his hands and drank noisily. He drank it all and finished with a sigh. She gave him a halfpenny. "Don't tell your Da that poor Auntie has to take medicine, he'd be vexed to hear it. Now go and gather your cinders."

Later he returned with an almost empty bucket and found Aunt Suzanne snoring on the sofa. He started to sing loudly so as to waken her, and she got up and vigorously poked the fire which the sun had almost put out.

"Give's a penny for the pictures?"

"If I had a penny I'd frame it, and you with no cinders."

"Go'n," he whimpered, "or I'll tell me Da about your medicine."

"Get out of my sight! Do you think I'm made of money!" she said crossly, watching the dust from the fire settling on the mantelpiece.

"Go'n!"

She lifted the poker in anger, and Arthur raced into the yard. He barricaded himself in an old hen-shed and started to sing:

> Boiled beef and carrots,
> Boiled beef and carrots,
> And porter for Suzanne."

He was innocent of the cruel implication, but it riled Auntie Sue, and she hammered at the door with the poker and flung jugfuls of water in at him through the slits in the boards. "The divil has the hold of you, me boyo! Wait'll your Da hears this and you'll catch it!"

He yelled louder; and, thinking of the neighbours, she went in and left him. He heard the bar shoot with finality in the scullery door and her last words: "You'll not get in the night! Go on, now, about your business."

All the evening he was in the dumps and sat far out on the waste ground at the back of the house. Annie and Mary came out with sweets in their hands and coaxed him in, assuring him that Auntie Sue was not going to touch him. And sure enough she had a Paris bun for his tea and jam on his bread. Then she stroked his head, kissed him, and packed him off to bed early.

That night the father returned to the nightly ritual of family prayers, which had been upset by the arrival of Suzanne in their midst. All knelt except Auntie Sue, who sat on a low chair with her rosary beads twined round one hand, the other resting on her lap. She closed her eyes as she answered the responses, and when she opened them there was always something to distract her: a new seat needed in Daniel's trousers, a stitch needed in Annie's dress. Then she fell to dreaming as she gazed at Mary's two plaits, tied at the ends with green ribbon — hair like her poor mother, God rest her. And then Annie's one plait with a broken ivory clasp — that's what she'd buy them at Christmas, two nice clasps, and maybe brooches with their names on them. A creak from Daniel's chair brought her mind back with a start, and she asked God to forgive her for such distraction as she turned to her beads again. But when he said solemnly: "All now repeat the Heroic Offering after me," she felt weak, and her heart pounded so loudly she thought they would all hear it.

For Thy greater glory and consolation, O Sacred Heart of Jesus . . . God forgive me for telling lies to that saintly man . . . *For Thy sake to give good example* . . . and wee Arthur saw me swilling it . . . *To practice self-denial* . . . and me with a bottle under a board in the room . . . *To make reparation to Thee for the sins of intemperance and the conversion of excessive drinkers* . . . God forgive me, God forgive me for being a hypocrite! I can't repeat the next of it . . . *I promise to abstain from all intoxicating drinks for life.*

She listened to the end of it with tightened lips, afraid to profane the sacred words, and thankful for the way the children almost shouted it. And later she was glad to get into the com-

forting darkness of her room, where she lay twisting and turning for a long time before sleep came to her.

After that she was cautious and always had a secret drink
behind a locked door, and kept bottles under a loose floor-board.
It was Arthur she feared: he was always appearing at surprising
moments stalking her, playing at Indians, pretending to himself
that she was a squaw on horseback, her iron-ring reminding him
of a stirrup. But Annie and Mary were the sensible children!
They looked forward to Arthur's bedtime, for with their father
at some Sodality meeting they had their Auntie to themselves.
They would ply her with questions about her schooldays, and
about Armagh and the games she played when she was young.
And Auntie sitting on the sofa between them, Annie hugging
one arm and Mary the other, would turn to one and then the
other, looking down at their anxious eyes as she told them
scraps about her life. Before Daniel would come in she would
sing for them verse after verse of *Lady Mouse*.

> "Lady Mouse, are you within?
> Hm, hm-m-m-m-m-m-m-m-m.
> Lady Mouse, are you within?
> Yes, kind sir, as she sat and spun,
> Hm, hm-m-m-m-m-m-m-m-m-m."

They had it by heart now, and all three hummed the hm-ms that
ended each verse. Sometimes the hm-ms would be so prolonged
by Annie or Mary till one or other would burst out laughing,
and Auntie would hold her sides: "I'll be kilt laughing, I'll be
kilt."

She sang for them songs of the countryside, courting songs
and songs of Ireland's heroes and Ireland's traitors, and some-

times she gave them riddles and phrases to say quickly: "Three grey geese in a green full of grazing, grey were the geese and green was the grazing." She taught them how to knit and how to crochet, and of a Sunday she would read to them out of her prayer book, and though the print was as big as that in a child's primer, she always followed the words with her finger.

In the long November nights, when the pains would come into her legs she would go off to bed early, and then Annie and Mary would come slipping into the room with a mug of hot tea for her and two big slices of griddle bread. They would light the candle and sit on the edge of the bed. While Auntie would be sipping the tea and dipping the bread in it, her eyes would travel round the holy pictures that she had tacked to the wall. "I have a quare squad of them around me, and there's none of them like that fella there," she would say, pointing to a picture of St. Patrick banishing the snakes. "A decent fella, a real gentleman, many's a good turn he done me."

Up through the long winter nights she drank little, and now and again at the family prayers she was on the verge of promising to abstain for life, but something told her she'd never keep it. Christmas came and she taught the children how to make a plum pudding; and she bought them brooches like her own with the words *Annie* and *Mary* in silver-white stones, and for Arthur a tram-conductor's cap and a ticket-puncher.

Then one cold winter's day when the snow had fallen and Annie and Mary had gone for messages, Auntie Sue was in the house alone. The coalman hadn't come, and there was only a fistful of cinders for the fire. She felt cold. She closed all the doors, but still there seemed to slice through every crevice in the house a wicked, icy draught. Her teeth chattered and she lifted the wrinkled quilt off her bed and put it round her

shoulders, looking miserably through the kitchen window at the white street and the light fading from the sky. Her thin blood craved for a drop of warmth — and not as much as a thimbleful of "medicine" in the house to wet her lips or make a drop of punch. Without waiting to talk it over in her mind, she left four shillings on the kitchen table for the coalman, put on her black plush coat and hat, took an umbrella, and out with her.

The hard snow lay deep in the street, yellowed by cart-ruts and blackened by coal-dust. In the sky a few stars were coming out. She put up her umbrella, though the snow wasn't falling. She passed neighbours cleaning their doorways with shovels, and now and again heard the wet, sad sloosh of a brush. A few snowballs thubbed on top of her umbrella and she hurried on, her iron-ring cutting circles in the snow. Then Arthur came running up with a snowball in his hand and she blew his nose for him and gave him a penny to buy sweets for himself. She turned the corner on to the main road, saw rags of snow cling-ing to the wheels of a cart, and the rich glow on a coalman's face as he lit his swinging lamp. The snow slushed in her boot and she shivered.

She went into The Bee Hive and sat in a snug near the stove. There was dry sawdust on the floor, a smell of new varnish, and a great glow of heat. She'd have a nice drop of punch. She held out her hands to the heat and smiled sweetishly as she heard the tight scringe of a cork coming out of a bottle.

That night the children were long in bed and Auntie Sue had not returned. Daniel was seated on the sofa in the firelight, a pair of his trousers drying on the back of a chair, the children's wet boots in a row on the fender. A quilt of snow fell from the roof into the yard. A knock came to the front door. Daniel lit the gas, and when he opened the door there was Aunt Suzanne hanging between the arms of two men. They linked her into the kitchen and on to the sofa, her skirt and coat dripping wet, her hat feathered with snow. She sang to herself pieces of *Lady Mouse* and began to hum. "Three gay grease," she said. "No, that's not it. Poor Auntie Sue can't say, 'Thee geese geen.' . . ."

Daniel stood in the middle of the floor staring with rising anger at the miserable woman on the sofa. She looked up at him with half-shut eyes and mumbled: "As dacent a man as ever walked in shoe-leather."

He went into her room and bundled all the things he could find into her band-box. He opened the door and looked up and down the street. A gramophone was playing and a child crying. The snow was falling and drifting quietly on to the window sills and the shut doors. Over the white, silent roofs the cold sky was sprayed with stars. A man with bowed head passed and said: "That's a hardy night," and Daniel heard him knock the snow off his boots and close his door. He came inside. Auntie Sue had leaned back on the sofa, her hands listless, her eyes shut. He took his trousers from the back of the chair, threw an overcoat over the huddled figure, and put out the gas.

In the morning Auntie Sue was leaving, and they all went down on the tram to see her off; Arthur knelt on the seat looking out, and no one chastised him when he pursed his lips against the window. They spoke little. They could find no words to say to each other.

At the station, before getting into the carriage, Aunt Suzanne gave him a penny, and her eyes were wet as she held Annie's and Mary's hands and stroked them lovingly. They couldn't look up at her, but stood awkwardly swaying to and fro. The train slid out and they lifted their arms and waved them wearily, tears filling their eyes. Arthur stood watching the back of the receding train. Then he plucked at Mary's coat. "Come, on quick," he said, but they didn't seem to hear him, and he ran on in front to the chocolate machine with the penny Auntie Sue had given him.

The Poteen Maker

WHEN he taught me about fifteen years ago he was an old man near his retirement, and when he would pass through the streets of the little town on his way from school you would hear the women talking about him as they stood at their doors knitting or nursing their babies: "Poor man, he's done . . . . . Killing himself . . . . . Digging his own grave!" With my bag of books under my arm I could hear them, but I could never understand why they said he was digging his own grave, and when I would ask my mother she would scold me: "Take your dinner, like a good boy, and don't be listening to the hard backbiters of this town. Your father has always a good word for Master Craig — so that should be enough for you!"

"But why do they say he's killing himself?"

"Why do who say? Didn't I tell you to take your dinner and not be repeating what the idle gossips of this town are saying. Listen to me, son! Master Craig is a decent, good-living man — a kindly man that would go out of his way to do you a good turn. If Master Craig was in any other town he'd have got a place in the new school at the Square instead of being stuck for ever in that wee poky bit of a school at the edge of the town!"

It was true that the school was small — a two-roomed ramshackle of a place that lay at the edge of the town beyond the last street lamp. We all loved it. Around it grew a few trees, their trunks hacked with boys' names and pierced with nibs and rusty drawing-pins. In summer when the windows were open we could hear the leaves rubbing together and in winter see the raindrops hanging on the bare twigs.

It was a draughty place and the master was always complaining of the cold, and even in the early autumn he would wear his overcoat in the classroom and rub his hands together: "Boys, it's very cold to-day. Do you feel it cold?" And to please him we would answer: "Yes, sir, 'tis very cold." He would continue to rub his hands and he would look out at the old trees casting their leaves or at the broken spout that flung its tail of rain against the window. He always kept his hands clean and three times a day he would wash them in a basin and wipe them on a roller towel affixed to the inside of his press. He had a hanger for his coat and a brush to brush away the chalk that accumulated on the collar in the course of the day.

In the wet, windy month of November three buckets were placed on the top of the desks to catch the drips that plopped here and there from the ceiling, and those drops made different music according to the direction of the wind. When the buckets were filled the master always called me to empty them, and I would take them one at a time and swirl them into the drain at the street and stand for a minute gazing down at the wet roofs of the town or listen to the rain pecking at the lunch-papers scattered about on the cinders.

"What's it like outside?" he always asked when I came in with the empty buckets.

"Sir, 'tis very bad."

He would write sums on the board and tell me to keep an eye on the class, and out to the porch he would go and stand in grim silence watching the rain nibbling at the puddles. Sometimes he would come in and I would see him sneak his hat from the press and disappear for five or ten minutes. We would fight then with rulers or paper-darts till our noise would disturb the mistress next door and in she would come and stand with her lips compressed, her finger in her book. There was silence as she upbraided us: "Mean, low, good-for-nothing corner boys. Wait'll Mister Craig comes back and I'll let him know the angels he has. And I'll give him special news about *you!*" — and she shakes her book at me: "An altar boy on Sunday and a corner boy for the rest of the week!" We would let her barge away, the buckets plink-plonking as they filled up with rain and her own class beginning to hum now that she was away from them.

When Mr. Craig came back he would look at us and ask if we disturbed Miss Lagan. Our silence or our tossed hair always gave him the answer. He would correct the sums on the board, flivell the pages of a book with his thumb, and listen to us reading; and occasionally he would glance out of the side-window at the river that flowed through the town and, above it, the bedraggled row of houses whose tumbling yard-walls sheered to the water's edge. "The loveliest county in Ireland is County Down!" he used to say, with a sweep of his arm to the river and the tin cans and the chalked walls of the houses.

During that December he was ill for two weeks and when he came back amongst us he was greatly failed. To keep out the draughts he nailed perforated plywood over the ventilators and stuffed blotting paper between the wide crevices at the jambs of the door. There were muddy marks of a ball on one of the windows and on one pane a long crack with fangs at the end of it: "So someone has drawn the River Ganges while I was away," he said; and whenever he came to the geography of

India he would refer to the Ganges delta by pointing to the cracks on the pane.

When our ration of coal for the fire was used up he would send me into the town with a bucket, a coat over my head to keep off the rain, and the money in my fist to buy a stone of coal. He always gave me a penny to buy sweets for myself, and I can always remember that he kept his money in a waistcoat pocket. Back again I would come with the coal and he would give me disused exercise books to light the fire. "Chief stoker!" he called me, and the name has stuck to me to this day.

It was at this time that the first snow had fallen, and someone by using empty potato bags had climbed over the glass-topped wall and stolen the school coal, and for some reason Mr. Craig did not send me with the bucket to buy more. The floor was continually wet from our boots, and our breaths frosted the windows. Whenever the door opened a cold draught would rush in and gulp down the breath-warmed air in the room. We would jig our feet and sit on our hands to warm them. Every half-hour Mr. Craig would make us stand and while he lilted *O'Donnell Abu* we did a series of physical exercises which he had taught us, and in the excitement and the exaltation we forgot about our sponging boots and the snow that pelted against the windows. It was then that he did his lessons on Science; and we were delighted to see the bunsen burner attached to the gas bracket which hung like an inverted T from the middle of the ceiling. The snoring bunsen seemed to heat up the room and we all gathered round it, pressing in on top of it till he scattered us back to our places with the cane: "Sit down!" he would shout. "There's no call to stand. Everybody will be able to see!"

The cold spell remained, and over and over again he repeated one lesson in Science, which he called: *Evaporation and Condensation*.

"I'll show you how to purify the dirtiest of water," he had told us. "Even the filthiest water from the old river could be made fit for drinking purposes." In a glass trough he had a dark brown liquid and when I got his back turned I dipped my finger in it and it tasted like treacle or burnt candy, and then I remembered about packets of brown sugar and tins of treacle I had seen in his press.

He placed some of the brown liquid in a glass retort and held it aloft to the class: "In the retort I have water which I have discoloured and made impure. In a few minutes I'll produce from it the clearest of spring water." And his weary eyes twinkled, and although we could see nothing funny in that, we smiled because he smiled.

The glass retort was set up with the flaming bunsen underneath, and as the liquid was boiling, the steam was trapped in a long-necked flask upon which I sponged cold water. With our eyes we followed the bubbling mixture and the steam turning into drops and dripping rapidly into the flask. The air was filled with a biscuity smell, and the only sound was the snore of the bunsen. Outside was the cold air and the falling snow. Presently the master turned out the gas and held up the flask containing the clear water.

"As pure as crystal!" he said, and we watched him pour some of it into a tumbler, hold it in his delicate fingers, and put it to his lips. With wonder we watched him drink it and then our eyes travelled to the dirty, cakey scum that had congealed on the glass sides of the retort. He pointed at this with his ruler: "The impurities are sifted out and the purest of pure water remains." And for some reason he gave his roguish smile. He filled up the retort again with the dirty brown liquid and repeated the experiment until he had a large bottle filled with the purest of pure water.

The following day it was still snowing and very cold. The master filled up the retort with the clear liquid which he had stored in the bottle: "I'll boil this again to show you that there are no impurities left." So, once again we watched the water bubbling, turning to steam, and then to shining drops. Mr. Craig filled up his tumbler: "As pure as crystal," he said, and then the door opened and in walked the Inspector. He was muffled to the ears and snow covered his hat and his attaché case. We all stared at him — he was the old, kind man whom we had seen before. He glanced at the bare firegrate and at the closed windows with their sashes edged with snow. The water continued to bubble in the retort, giving out its pleasant smell.

The Inspector shook hands with Mr. Craig and they talked and smiled together, the Inspector now and again looking towards the empty grate and shaking his head. He unrolled his scarf and flicked the snow from off his shoulders and from his attaché case. He sniffed the air, rubbed his frozen hands together, and took a black notebook from his case. The snow ploofed against the windows and the wind hummed under the door.

"Now, boys," Mr. Craig continued, holding up the tumbler of water from which a thread of steam wriggled in the air. He talked to us in a strange voice and told us about the experiment as if we were seeing it for the first time. Then the Inspector took the warm tumbler and questioned us on our lesson. "It should be perfectly pure water," he said, and he sipped at it. He tasted its flavour. He sipped at it again. He turned to Mr. Craig. They whispered together, the Inspector looking towards the retort which was still bubbling and sending out its twirls of steam to be condensed to water of purest crystal. He laughed loudly, and we smiled when he again put the tumbler to his lips and this time drank it all. Then he asked us more questions and told us how, if we were shipwrecked, we could make pure water from the salt-sea water.

Mr. Craig turned off the bunsen and the Inspector spoke to him. The master filled up the Inspector's tumbler and poured out some for himself in a cup. Then the Inspector made jokes with us, listened to us singing, and told us we were the best class in Ireland. Then he gave us a few sums to do in our books. He put his hands in his pockets and jingled his money, rubbed a little peep-hole in the breath-covered window and peered out at the loveliest sight in Ireland. He spoke to Mr. Craig again and Mr. Craig shook hands with him and they both laughed. The Inspector looked at his watch. Our class was let out early, and while I remained behind to tidy up the Science apparatus the master gave me an empty treacle tin to throw in the bin and told me to carry the Inspector's case up to the station. I remember that day well as I walked behind them through the snow, carrying the attaché case, and how loudly they talked and laughed as the snow whirled cold from the river. I remember how they crouched together to light their cigarettes, how match after match was thrown on the road, and how they walked off with the unlighted cigarettes still in their mouths. At the station Mr. Craig took a penny from his waistcoat pocket and as he handed it to me it dropped on the snow. I lifted it and he told me I was the best boy in Ireland . . . . .

When I was coming from his funeral last week — God have mercy on him — I recalled that wintry day and the feel of the cold penny and how much more I know now about Mr. Craig than I did then. On my way out of the town — I don't live there now — I passed the school and saw a patch of new slates on the roof and an ugly iron barrier near the door to keep the home-going children from rushing headlong on to the road. I knew if I had looked at the trees I'd have seen rusty drawing-pins stuck into their rough flesh. But I passed by. I heard there was a young teacher in the school now, with an array of coloured pencils in his breast pocket.

Look at the Boats

"OH, Sister, look at the boats!" The boy pointed at the docks where red funnels of ships rose in the air, the wintry sun shining on their varnished masts.

"You'll see plenty of boats, Peter, where you are going. Come quickly now or you'll miss the train," said the nun, walking along with her head down and her hands in her sleeves.

Around them was the pulse and traffic of the city, but Peter paid no heed as he began to spell aloud the enormous black letters printed on the shipping sheds: G-L-A-S-G-O-W, L-I-V-E-R-P-O-O-L, H-E-Y-S-H-A-M.

They came on to the iron-latticed bridge and in sight of the station. The nun walked slowly, allowing Peter to enjoy the grand view of the boats from the bridge. The harbour was blue and sparkled with cold sunlight, but under the bridge the water was brown and carried on its back whirls of soot and orange peel. Peter leaned over the parapet, fascinated by the long line of ships and the gulls that flew around them.

Over the bridge they went. A one-legged man sat beside his charcoal drawings and a few coppers lay in his cap, but Peter had no eyes for him; he kept craning his head towards the ships, and when he came into the chilly station he could see them no more.

"Don't you worry, madam," said the railway guard to the nun.
"I'll see him right to Downpatrick."

The nun placed a hand on Peter's shoulder: "Be a good boy
now and work hard for your new master." And as she passed
out of the station she sighed: "They're getting a manly little
fellow anyway."

Peter, carrying his belongings in a brown parcel, walked
along the platform, and the guard opened a carriage door for
him: "Sit in there, and don't be sticking yer head out of the
window. She'll be going out in a minute or two."

The carriage was heated, the windows closed, and a stale
tobacco smell lingering in the air. He sat down on the seat
with the parcel on his lap, and waited for the train to start.

He was a sturdy lad of fifteen, black haired, dressed in a
grey suit and grey stockings; and swivelled to a button on his
coat was a label with his new address printed in ink:

> PETER McCLOSKEY,
>> c/o. MR. & MRS. ROBERT GILL,
>>> KILLARD,
>>>> STRANGFORD, CO. DOWN.

He was fingering the label when the guard came in and told
him about the people he was going to: "Aw, Robert Gill is as
dacent a man as you'll find in the whole countryside. He'll be
at Downpatrick to meet you . . . . . . Aw, you'll have a nice
place with Robert."

Slowly the train moved out, and sunlight crossed and re-
crossed the carriage like pages turning in a book. Out past the
backs of grey houses it rumbled and he saw chalk-markings on
the doors, pigeon-sheds on the yard walls, a clothes-line with
two pegs, and in one place the paper tails of a kite entangled
in the telegraph wires. Stations with tin advertisements rattled

past, and then came a great brightness in the carriage as the train raced into the open country.

The hedges were black and ragged, and deserted nests stuck out as clear as thrown sods. The fields were newly ploughed, and around the farm houses were hay stacks and bare trees. Sheep rushed madly from the thundering train; the long twisted roll of smoke shook itself over the fields, tore through the hedges, and trailed away in tattered rags.

Here and there at a station groups of shawled women with baskets waited for the train, and sometimes the guard opened Peter's door: "Everything all right, lad? It won't be long now till we're there." He would wave his green flag and the train, with many a protesting grunt, would chug away from the silent box of a station.

The country became more hummocky, and from the window he saw the lovely triangular mountains of Mourne. Presently the train curved and rumbled between rushy lakes that were littered with wild duck. And suddenly the ducks arose and circled in great scattered flocks until the noise of the train was swallowed up in Downpatrick station.

Peter sat patiently in the carriage; doors opened and slammed; and then the guard appeared, accompanied by a small man smoking a pipe.

"This is your lad, Robert. A fine lump of a fella he looks!"

Robert nodded his head and shook Peter's hand. They passed out of the station, Robert a little in front, the tail of his green-black overcoat spattered with mud, and a tweed cap on the back of his head. They went over to a cart where a woman stood at the horse's head.

"Alice!" Robert said to her. "This is our boy . . . . . What's this now yer name is? . . . . . Peter! A good solid name! 'Thou art

Peter and upon this Rock' . . . . . Man, I knew my catechism
when I was at school. And do ye know, the schoolmaster wanted
me to go on for the Church . . . . ."

"Here quit the swaggering till we get on the road," interrupted Alice. "The boy's perished with the cold. I'm sure you're
hungry, son . . . . . Come on, Robert, and we'll go over to Fitz-
simon's atin'-house for a mouthful of tay."

They crossed to a shop that displayed in the window dishes
of soda farls and four bottles of lemonade, a flower-pot with no
flowers, and a card announcing in scraggy letters: TEA,
BREAD, and BUTTER — 6d.

When they came out again, the faint sun was low in the sky,
a frosty wind was skimming over the road, and the horse was
stamping impatiently. They moved slowly out of the hilly town,
Robert and Alice walking alongside the cart, and Peter sitting
in it with a black shawl pinned around his shoulders. Up and up
they climbed, with Downpatrick, a grey town of hills and
hollows, clumped behind them. The sun had now exhausted
itself, and its light shone on the ploughed land and the gables
of white cottages.

They topped the braes and descended towards flat-spreading
land with the long arm of Strangford Lough stretching into it.
Robert motioned with his pipe to a white column that marked
the mouth of the lough and the open sea. "Fornenst that is the
house, Peter. We're down at the very jaws of the sea!" And he
shook the rope-reins of the horse and she moved quickly down
the hill. He looked at his big watch and then turned his head
towards the lowering sun: "It'll be dark afore we're home." And
he handed the reins to Alice and pared a stump of a candle for
the lamp. His hands were red with the cold and when he shut
his fists white marks appeared on his knuckles.

The cart bumped and jolted on the road. A cold wind swept over the land and the candle brightened in the increasing darkness. The horse began to pull harder and a brisker sound rattled from her hooves as she came into the full blast of the sea. The land was now dark and lights from the scattered homes glimmered like little sparks; Peter could see them through the bare hedges and sometimes his eyes shut as he gazed at the shadows of the wheel revolving in the light of the lamp. But when he heard the waves break on the stones he sat up alert and occupied, gazing across the black land to the steely sea.

The horse stopped and Robert stretched himself and groaned: "Thank God, we're landed!"

The key was turned in the door, and Alice, without taking off her hat and coat, went cautiously over to the oil-lamp on the wall, and when it was lit Peter saw the interior of his new home. The fire was out, the floor was stone flagged, a towel hung from a nail on the back door, and above it was a horseshoe covered with silver paper.

Robert stamped about and rubbed his hands: "That night's as dark as a grave. Hurry up, Alice, and get a blink in the fire."

Then he began to spar playfully with Peter. "Man, boy, when I was at sea I was a great fighter. I mind once when we landed at Bombay and one of them Indian coolies — aw, a towering giant of a fella — he starts to give up ould guff."

"Here!" ordered Alice. "Will you stop your ould guff and hack a bit of stick for the fire . . . . . Here, child! He wouldn't think of offering you a seat itself with his ould blether. Sit over at the hearth, though there's no fire in it 'tis warmer than around the door."

Peter sat on the stool. Above him were black rafters with rows of salted fish and coils of rope, and in one corner an old

checked school-bag which caught his eye every time he raised
his head.

Soon the sticks were crackling and Robert, with his overcoat
around him and his cap pushed back from his bald head, took
a chair by the fire. He began to light his pipe and Peter watched
the glow on his brown face and his eyes shining as dark as sloes.
He pulled deeply at the pipe and pressed the lighted paper
down into the bowl.

"Do ye know," says he, without taking his eyes off the bowl
of the pipe, "what is the nearest thing to death about a house?"

Nobody answered him and he made another spill to light his
pipe. "Well, I'll tell ye . . . . . A hearth without a fire and a house
without a woman!"

He spat into the fire with great satisfaction and swayed back
on the chair till its front legs rode off the floor.

Alice listened to him and her mind stumbled back through
the years, and from the tangles of her memory she sought for
the things that had been her life: marrying Robert when he
came from sea; buying the house and the land; black winters
and poor harvests that they had lived through; and now when
old age had crept upon them they had brought in a boy to help
with the land and the fishing. She turned and saw him with his
hands on his knees, her shawl around his shoulders and the pin
of it catching the firelight. She sighed to herself: "The years are
flying." And as if to hold them back and get something done
she bustled so quickly about the table that Robert looked at
her with pride. "Man, Alice, you're the girl can hustle herself
when hunger's in the air."

Peter sat quite still. Outside was the noising sea, and he
thought of the boats that he had seen in the morning, his leaving the orphanage with the nun, the train and the guard, and

then the tiresome journey on the cart. It seemed such a long, long time for one day.

"Now, Peter, eat yer fill. Butter his bread for him, Alice . . . . . Them newspapers tell ye not to eat goin' to bed. But don't heed them. Always take plenty of ballast aboard for a night's journey."

Alice smiled and he noticed that she was eating nothing. "Are yer pains back again, Alice?"

"No, no, the journey's upset me," and she split a farl in two and forced herself to eat.

After the tea Peter drowsed by the fire, listening to the slow contented pulls of Robert's pipe and Alice making a yellow mash for the hens. Then the sounds became blurred, his eyes closed, and his head jerked towards the fire.

"Yer dying with sleep, Peter!" and Robert stretched out a hand and patted his knee.

He smiled sleepily, and Alice lit a candle and brought him across the kitchen to his room. The air was cold, the bed low, and boxes and trunks along the walls. She thumped the pillow a few times and then drew in her breath sharply as a pain stabbed her side. Peter looked at her anxiously and she smiled. "Good-night now, and don't forget yer prayers. And blow out the candle."

He lay for awhile listening to the sea; and later when Alice peeped into the room to see if he had blown out the candle he was fast asleep.

In the morning, instead of the white enamel bed of the orphanage and the noisy chatter of boys, he found himself in a dark little room. Coats with newspapers on the shoulders hung on the door and gulls flew past the window. A bucket clattered and Alice shouted: "Away on, you thief . . . . . . There's that

rogue of a gull back again, Robert. I can't leave a pick of hens'
mate about the place but she throttles it!"

Robert stamped his feet at the threshold.

"I'll lame her one of these fine days! That's the same girl that
lifts the salted fish! Ai, I'll give it to her!" The gull called and
dipped low over the house and a fistful of gravel followed in
her wake.

Every morning there was the same taunt, but the gulls paid
no heed and flocked around unconcernedly. The days were
short and cold. The white cottage with its tarred roof over-
looked the sea, and in stormy weather the spray flung itself at
the windows, swished on the roof, and the gulls forsook the
shore.

Slowly Peter fitted into his new life, and he would often sit
with Robert on the upturned boat at the side of the house. The
boat was propped on flat stones and made a shelter for the
hens in wet weather; and one day when Peter himself had
crawled under it Robert had seen him and shouted in to him:
"Look hard and tell me if ye see any seams of light in her roof."
And when Peter had answered "No!" Robert began to praise the
great timber that was in her and to tell Peter of the grand fishing they'd have as soon as June arrived.

It was now March, the days dry and blustery, and the sea
very blue. Robert's land was ready for the plough and one dry
morning he and Peter were early astir. They went out to a last
year's potato field which lay grey and uneven under a cold sky.

The plough tore it up without bother. Peter walked in front
of the plough and lifted stones out of its way, while behind
Alice gathered in her lap potatoes that had lain in the soil all
winter. Day by day Peter learned Robert's phrases: "There's no
nourishment in land that's easily ploughed," or "The soil here'd

kill no horse: it's too dry and sandy," or "It's a hungry bit of land and you have to keep feedin' it with manure." And Peter repeated these to himself and to the boys he met in the evenings or coming from Mass.

When the field was opened Robert began to sow the seed using a bed-sheet looped around his neck as a carrier. He sowed the one way, scattering the grain with his back to the wind for it was blowing fiercely. Peter stood to the side clodding at the gulls and the crows and pouring buckets of seed into the sheet. The small field was at the back of the house and sheltered from the sea by a scraggy line of thorn bushes; they were now stooped and black, and from their lower thorns sheep's wool streamed in the wind. To keep himself warm Peter raced and shouted at the birds, and even when Alice called him for his dinner he looked angrily out of the window at the crows waddling over the brown soil and pecking at the seed. "Them's the thieves; they'll have all the corn ate if we don't hurry."

"Aw now, they have to feed like everybody else," Robert winked at Alice.

But Peter rose from his dinner and with his fists full of stones he made out to the field and scatterd the gulls and the crows. The next day Robert let him harrow and laughed at the way he sprawkled over the soil. "Aw, Peter, yer not strong enough. But ye'll grow, and next year ye'll be sowing the grain yerself."

Cold days passed and the brown field was swept by a frosty wind. Then came rain and the green shoots appeared above the ground. Buds came in the thorn bushes, but no birds sang in them. And one day when Robert saw Peter searching for nests he nodded his head. "Them bushes are poisoned with the salt water and there's no shelter in them. It's in from the sea the birds build," and he pointed across his fields to the thick hedges and the clumps of trees that rose out of kindlier land.

Whins came in bloom, the larks rose in the air, and the ewes gave birth to their young. It was time for putting in potatoes. People were in the fields from early morning and in the evenings the dead weeds were burnt and the air was filled with a pleasant smell.

Robert's potato field was small and his own horse opened the drills. The seed potatoes were carried out in crates from the dark barn. Peter forked the manure into the furrows and Alice placed the seed on top with their white teeth towards the sky. The plough moved down and the soil gushed over the seed. In two days they had sown the potatoes; and then Robert made lobster-pots, Peter sitting beside him on the upturned boat learning the craft.

For weeks the wind stayed in the north and there came no rain. The soil turned grey and the young corn ceased growing. At Mass on Sunday they offered up prayers for rain and on the road home Robert joked with the neighbours: "The Man above is tired listening to us. His head is astray with our crankiness. When it does rain we want sunshine and when we have sun we want rain."

But the days continued dry and warm, and Peter had to take the horse to a river a mile off and cart home barrels of water. The sun scorched the land, and the seedlings lengthened their white roots and sought strength and moisture in the darker earth. And in the evenings Robert stood at the gable of the house looking across the land at the sun going down in yellow glory from the naked sky.

Then the wind changed to the south and the air became soft with the promise of rain. Flocks of black cloud blew in from the sea and from their ragged edges rain fell like tails of sand. The soil softened, wet mists lay in the folds of the land, and in the evenings there was the smell of growing things.

The grass thickened and Peter had to take the cow along the sea-road and let it graze from the banks. Alice gave him a switch and when he went into the byre to fetch the cow Robert followed him. "If the policeman passing on his bicycle asks ye why the cow is trespassin' on the public highway tell him yer takin' her to the field. Do ye hear?" And he laughed loudly for he knew there wasn't as much grazing in his field as'd satisfy a goat.

As the cow grazed along the edges of the road Peter ran down the sloping bank to the shore and searched for crabs; and amongst the hard encrusted seaweed he found whitened corks and rusted tin-tops of bottles, and with these he made a boat with funnels and decks. He lay and watched the tide, like a river in flood, flowing out of the lough to the open sea. And one day when a coal-boat approached he forgot about the cow, so intensely did the boat hold his mind. It cruised about the bar waiting for the tide to turn and carry it up to Portaferry; then as it neared the shore he gazed at the white spurt of water that gushed from its side and at the smoke purling from the funnel. A man in his shirt-sleeves leaned over the rail and flung a bucket with a rope on it into the sea, and then he hauled in and swilled the water along the deck. Peter waited for him to do it again, but the hoot of a lorry startled him and he raced up to the narrow road where the driver abused him for having his cow loose.

Every day, now, he was to be seen with the cow along the road; and the neighbours got to know him and bade him the time of day, as they passed in carts, on bicycles, or on foot. He learned the directions of the wind, and when it blew soft and

moist from the south-west and he saw in the distance the clouds pile up on the top of the Mournes he knew it was going to rain. But he never turned home. He sought shelter at the gables of tumbled-down houses or snuggled against grassy banks, knowing that the wind blew strong from the sea and slanted the rain from him. At such times he tore out stones from the bank and prodded the scurrying ants with a twig as they scrambled into their tiny holes. Then he would watch the gulls on the shore all facing windward and he knew they did that to keep their feathers smooth. Sometimes he gathered primroses and put them in a glass jam-pot in the ledge of the window; and once when he was gathering them a lark flew off her nest and he saw her five chocolate eggs, and watched day by day until the young birds had feathered and taken wing.

In the evenings shelduck flew in flocks from the upper reaches of the lough and fed amongst the weedy stones and green glut below the house. He often tried to get near them, but they were always first to fly off and alight again on the other side of the lough. Lazily the gulls would follow, and the shore would be deserted when Peter had gone back to the house. As darkness fell he would stand at the bedroom window, gazing at the windy light of the buoy on the lough's mouth and farther out the winking lights of ships passing through the night.

The summer came, the crops grew and hid the clay in the fields. Robert tarred and painted his boat, spread her brown sail in the sun and patched it in places where the mice had gnawed it. Hens' feathers stuck to the tar, the sun blistered it and Peter burst the blisters with his fingers. The day arrived when she was carried from the side of the house to the shore. Robert taught him how to row and how to feather his oar; and in the evenings he stood proudly at the door, feeling the hardness of his muscles, and looking at the boat lying up on the stones.

In the mornings they were up when the fields were grey with dew, the sea cold and colourless, and the sky dull. The whole world would be asleep but themselves and the sea. They spoke little to each other as Peter pulled towards the line of corks that marked the lobster pots. Robert, standing in the stern, would heave in the pots, cautiously take out the blue lobsters and then rebait with stale fish. The chilly air would fling the sleep from Peter, and resting on the oars he would scan that low, wide land with its white houses, dead and deserted, and nothing astir now but the beasts in the fields and an odd gull swaying in the air. Far out at sea the steamers, lonely and black, seemed to catch a deadness from the morning. But when the sun burst forth and flung a broken quivering light upon the sea, mist rose from the land, whiteness came to gulls, and the cows coughed as they got up from the crushed-warm grass.

" 'Tis the best time of the day to be up, Peter. You could thrive on that air; there's great strength in it," and Robert would smoke his pipe as he tied the toes of the lobsters with bits of string. "If you left them boyos too long in the pots they'd find their way out again; and you'd think to look at their ugly mugs that they'd no intelligence. But them big crabs! I don't think they could find their way out of an empty can!"

In again, Alice would have the fire going and bowls of hot tea and eggs on the table. And one morning when they had finished their breakfast Robert told Peter to get the spade, and at low tide they went off to dig in the sand for lug worm. "I'll bring you out to the banks this day and we'll give the whiting a quare scutching. Do ye think ye'd be fit to pull her out?"

"I could row her the whole way myself," Peter replied with great eagerness.

After the dinner Robert got ready the hand-lines and Alice filled a can with buttermilk and in another can put bread and scallions.

"This'll help to keep away the hunger till yiz come in again," and she handed the cans to Peter.

"And listen, Alice," said Robert turning at the door, "when Kelly comes round about the lobsters, don't be soft with him. Tell him my orders: a shillin' a-piece for the lobsters or no sale."

She watched them go down to the boat. Peter in front carrying the cans, and Robert with an oar under his arm and the fishing gear in a basket.

They rowed out to the mouth of the lough and when they reached the open sea they hoisted the sail. A few boats were already on the banks and when Robert saw them he said with great pride: "Them boats is too far south for this tide. Wait'll ye see where Robert'll anchor," and his eye scanned the coast. "We'll not be there till the boat's in line with the Mill and the Black Rock," and he pointed to the land and taught Peter the 'marks.'

"Go up to the bow, now, and pitch out the anchor when I tell ye." Robert jabbed at the water with his oars, his eyes fixed on the mainland. "Now!" he shouted.

Out went the anchor, and the rope burned through Peter's hands until the anchor found bottom. The boat swung round and bobbed up and down on the waves. A few gulls floated near and called loudly when the sun shone on them from a blue gap in the clouds.

Robert showed Peter how to bait the hooks, and in a few minutes the lead sinkers on the lines were flung over the side and were racing for the sandy bottom. They hauled in together

and Peter laughed with delight when he saw a whiting on each
of his hooks.

"And ye tell me ye never fished in yer life before . . . . Well,
well, it's hard to believe it. It must be in the blood . . . . . .
Ye'll see them other boats comin' over to us when they see how
we're killing . . . . . D'ye think ye could find it again?"

Peter faced the land. "Get the Mill and the Black Rock in line
with the boat and out with yer anchor!"

Robert laughed loudly at the way Peter answered him and
added: "Yer a purty intelligent fella . . . . . Ye must have
been born on the sea."

And so they lay out for hours, sometimes Robert smoking or
handing round the can of buttermilk and the bread. Peter loved
it and only wished now that he could smoke a pipe like Robert.
He watched the gannets bursting into the sea and the cor-
morants with their long necks flying near the surface, but when
the Ardglass herring boats appeared in the south he shouted
excitedly: "Look, Robert, at the long line of boats."

" 'Them's the Ardglass men going out in the heel of the
evening . . . . . It's a grand sight to see them . . . . . But it's
the Dutch boats ye want to see; a lovely sight with their
coloured sails. It's like a procession with banners."

Peter listened as he told about other parts of the world, but
all the time his eyes were on the herring drifters, watching the
distance shorten between them. "Are they tryin' a race, Robert?"

" 'Deed, by my sowl, they might be! But it's not always the
first boat gets the most herrin'."

They hauled in the anchor and moved to a fresh mark, and
when the sun had set they made for home. The evening was
without an air of wind and they had to row, Robert advising
Peter to take it easy as they had a long pull ahead of them. To

the left at the foot of the sky were the hills of the Isle of Man with a big steamer passing near.

"That boat's goin' to Liverpool from Belfast," said Robert; and Peter remembered the day he had spelt aloud the words on the shipping sheds.

"And are there many boats in Liverpool?" he asked.

"Aw, hould yer tongue!" Robert spat over the side. "They're as thick as the corn in the fields; they choke each other for space — boats from all parts of the world! That's a sight! It wasn't the first time Robert was in Liverpool. And d'ye know that's where I signed on my first boat."

He began to tell how he had left home for Belfast and sailed for Liverpool. He told of the foreign countries that he had seen, fights at sea, and how once in a fierce storm he was flung out of his bunk and had broken his arm.

Peter listened to him in silence.

"What d'ye think of that for a life?" Robert finished.

Peter startled, his eyes were shining, and he gave a nervous little laugh.

Behind them the beam from St. John's Lighthouse was lengthening in the wading dark. They rowed with long slow sweeps and soon they rounded the point and came into their own quiet bay. Alice had the light in the window and its beam made a shivering path upon the sea.

In below the house they landed and when Alice heard the thump of the oars she came down to meet them. She crossed her hands over her breast when she saw the white mass of fish.

"Well, yiz did get one or two."

Robert didn't answer her.

"And had you any luck, Peter?"

"Any luck!" And Robert told about the way Peter fished:

"In the line goes and up it comes — a pair of whiting on it every time."

Peter smiled and pulled with all his strength when they hauled the boat. There was silence; waves jabbled amongst the stones and a fish flapped in a last leap. Out on the bar the buoy's light shone and a chilly air rose up from the sea. Robert would roll up the sail, Peter bail out with a tin the brackish water, and together they would walk slowly towards the warm light in the doorway. Peter would chop sticks for the morning's fire and then take a last look round at the sheds. Sometimes he would stay out too long and Alice would come to the door: "Peter, are you there? Come on in or ye'll be foundered. There's a draught comes through the mouth of the lough that'd clean corn!"

And when the door was shut for the night, the blinds hooked to the window, the dishes washed and put on the dresser, Robert would take out his pipe, and Peter begin paring a piece of wood that was gradually taking on the shape of a boat. Alice would salt the fish and in the sunny mornings put them on the low hen-house roof and cover them with netting-wire.

Week by week their stock of fish increased; the corn ripened early and their potatoes were good. At night when Peter had gone to bed they'd sit close to the fire and talk about him and the year that was ending. "That boy has brought us great luck . . . . . Thanks be to God for him!" And they'd fall silent and feel a deep peace breathing in the house.

The winter was stormy. Robert nailed boards on the outside of the windows to break the force of the tide, the door was shut early, and great fires of coal banked high in the wide grate. If no neighbour had come in for a céilidhe Robert lifted down his old schoolbag and took out his black Reading Book. Its pages were yellow and gave off a damp mouldy smell. Across the flyleaf there was written in scraggy letters: ROBERT GILL, KILCLIEF NATIONAL SCHOOLS, 1880.

"I was a good hand-writer in them days," he said, "but my fingers is now buckled with age."

Peter got the book and was told to read aloud Robert's favourite lesson: *The Locusts* . . . . . *For twelve miles did they extend from front to rear, and their whizzing and hissing could be heard for six miles on every side of them. The bright sun, though hidden by them, illumined their bodies, and was reflected from their quivering wings; and as they fell heavily earthward, they seemed like the innumerable flakes of a yellow-coloured snow. The poor peasants hastily dug pits and trenches as their enemy came on, in vain they filled them from the wells or with lighted stubble. Heavily and thickly did the locusts fall; they were lavish of their lives: they choked the flame and the water, which destroyed them the while, and the vast living hostile armament still moved on* . . . . . .

"Them's the quare plague for you," Robert commented. "We have the blow-fly here and the cleg, but thanks be to God, we've no locusts. They'd make short work of our wee bit of land."

If Peter balked at a word Robert supplied it without consulting the book for he knew it as well as Alice knew her prayer book. Alice was knitting a blue gansey for Peter and sometimes she'd pause and say: "Is there nothing cheerful in that book? I'm tired of them sad stories." Then she'd go on with her work and call Peter over beside her and measure the jersey against his chest. "It's a bit on the short side yet."

"Give him plenty of room in it," Robert would put in, "for he's growin' like a bad weed and I must get him long trousers."

The evening the gansey was finished Robert measured Peter's leg with a string, and the next morning he went off in the cart to Downpatrick. That day Alice was feeding the fowl and Peter saw her sway and fall to the ground. He carried her into the house, sprinkled cold water on her face, and she opened her eyes and slowly smiled at him: "I'm a silly woman to be fallin' on ye like that. Ye mustn't tell Robert on me." But ever afterwards when Peter would gaze at her she'd smile and say: "What's wrong with ye the day, Peter, yer very quiet?" And at Mass on Sundays he noticed how she sat upon the seat and only knelt at the Consecration.

Coming home from Mass Robert and Peter walked together: Robert with the pipe in his mouth, and Peter with his thumbs stuck in his trousers' belt and his hob-nailed boots striking the road with great vigour.

He grew tall and strong and that spring he was able to hold the plough and put down a barbed wire fence to keep out the sheep. But the rabbits came into the young corn in spite of him, and one evening as they were setting snares Robert said to him: "They aren't as good as the frog."

"What frog?"

"Well, that's a good one," replied Robert, as he hammered a peg into the ground. "And ye tell me ye never heard of the frog. It bates all none of the lads or Alice told you about me and the frog."

He lit his pipe, stuffed his hands in his pockets and began to walk from the sandy banks towards the house. The light was in the window and the wind was stirring in the grass.

"There'll be a few rabbits in them in the morning, for a windy night brings them out on the prowl. Aw, if only we could catch a frog." And then he began to walk slowly. "It was a night like this, only calmer, when I came out my lone to get a rabbit or two. I mind it well, Peter. It was very dark and there wasn't a star to be seen anywhere and there wasn't as much wind in it as'd sway a cobweb. And when I reached the hollow over there I heard a frog croaking, and I crept over on my hands and knees and caught him. Then I takes out a stump of a candle, lights it, and splatters a few drops on the frog's back, and sticks my candle on top. What do I do now? Into the first rabbit hole I put my frog and in he hopped with the candle still flaring on top of his back.

"The rabbits must have thought it was the Day of Judgment, for they raced out of the holes, big ones and wee ones, old ones and young ones, fat ones and skinny ones, black ones and brown ones, and out by another hole came the frog and I could see him in the dark and the candle as bright as a torch. He was like a trained dog the way he hopped out of one hole into another. And the rabbits tore round me and I cracked out with my stick and the squeals of them could be heard in the Isle of Man. And then a breeze sprang up and I saw the candle go blind, and I never seen trace of my frog from that day till this. And the next morning I never seen the like of it for rabbits: they lay dead in their hundreds, some of them were paralysed for life, and them that got away took till the sea and for weeks the shores was covered with their carcasses. Cablegrams came from Australia asking me to name my price to banish their rabbits. I'd have went right away, but long journeys don't agree with Alice and so we stayed at home."

When he had finished his story Peter waited for him to laugh, but Robert smoked away, and the light of the pipe lit up his eyes and there was a seriousness in them as if he were thinking of something else.

The next day when Robert had taken the horse to the black-smith's, Peter questioned Alice about the frog.

"Don't heed what Robert tells you. He always blathers when he gets somebody to listen to him. He told me many's a one, but never that one . . . . . The only rabbit he ever brought in was an ould thing a motor ran over one winter's night."

"Well, was he at sea, Alice?"

" 'Deed, child, he wrought for whiles in Liverpool and was at sea for ten years. But it'd have taken him forty years to ramble the countries that he says he was in. Don't listen to him." And she went on with her work scrubbing the table and halting now and again to look out of the window at the green growth in the fields. She scrubbed vigorously and Peter smiled, remembering the day not long ago when she had fallen at the gable.

But one evening as they were making in from the fishing it was dark and there was a light in one of the bedrooms, and when they came ashore two women were there to meet them. "Alice is bad, Robert," one said, and he hurried up the sloping bank to the house, leaving Peter to moor the boat.

Alice was in bed and she smiled weakly at him when he entered the room. There was a bruise on her forehead where she had fallen in her weakness.

"I'll be all right in the morning," she said, and she raised her hand and it fell limply on the quilt.

In the morning she could see the lovely white clouds of May go sailing across the sky. The gulls flew around the window, and the cold, fresh smell of the sea blew into the room. She could hear Robert calling the hens or throwing out the dregs of the teapot on the causeway. She tried to sit up, but she fell back, and her breathing quickened.

Robert talked to her about little things that livened their

lives: "Do you mind the time, Alice, that the ould gypsy said you'd lose something soon? . . . . . Do you mind the time we had to fut it the whole way home from Crossgar? . . . . . "
Alice looked at him and shut her eyes. "Ah, Robert, my memory is wearin' as thin as an ould shoe."

Peter would come into the room and sit on the edge of the bed, and she'd stroke his hand. "Stay with me for a wee while, I be lonely when I hear no stir about the house."

The priest came. Two days afterwards she was brought to the Downpatrick Infirmary, and one morning about three o'clock a policeman on his bicycle rapped loudly at Robert's door and when he hurried out of bed to open it he knew that Alice was dead.

For days a gloom hung over the house; Robert was quiet in himself, and at night he would sit in the light of the fire. He sold the cow, for there'd be nobody to look after her or milk her when they'd be at the fishing.

But even at the fishing he was quiet and full of unrest, and as he pared his tobacco he'd say: "I declare to God the tobacco they make nowadays is not what it used to be," and he would hold out a chunk of it to Peter. "Smell that! D'ye not get an ould stale reek of it?" And before sundown he would order Peter to lift the anchor.

"But we've another hour or two yet," Peter would answer.

"Do as yer bid. We must get in afore dark. Lying out here like an ould plank that has nowhere to go!"

But one evening a head wind blew strong and they had to pull hard against it. It was pitch dark when they reached the little bay below the house. No light from the window warmed the sea, and looking up at it from the boat Robert said brokenly: "It's a lonesome looking place without a light . . . . . The house is dead!" And Peter saw something of the man's mind and remembered the first night he had stepped across the threshold and how Alice had lit the lamp on the wall.

Now it was changed. The house was chilly with no fire reddening the grate. Crusts discoloured by tea lay on the table and dirty dishes were pushed to the side. The floor was unswept and ashes were high in the grate.

Robert bent to a few sticks and began chopping.

"Sit down, Robert, and rest yerself and I'll light the fire."

"And d'ye think I'm not fit to light my own fire?" he answered crossly. "Fill the kettle with water if ye want a job and see that the hens are all in."

Robert stuck a lighted candle to an upturned bowl, placed it on the table, and sat down to the tea. He buttered a piece of bread for Peter. "Eat up now, for I like to see a growin' lad eat his fill . . . . . Ye'll have to make yer own in the mornin' for I'm going to Downpatrick."

And Robert went to his bed and lay awake, his mind disordered. He thought of Alice and prayed for her soul; he thought of Peter. "A brave lad, but if I show him he's too useful he'll override me. I must be firm with him."

In the other room Peter was standing at the window. A high moon had arrived in the sky and where it shone on the water he could see the rise and fall of the waves. Down on the beach was the boat, and a glint came from the bailing tin that lay beside it. Out at sea a big steamer passed with her port-holes all alight, and he watched them until they were swallowed up by the night.

In the morning he was up first and Robert was not astir. He lit the fire. It was past nine o'clock when Robert came into the kitchen, pulling his braces over his shoulders.

"Why didn't you call me, boy? Didn't ye know I was for Downpatrick?"

"I thought maybe ye'd changed yer mind."

"And how'd I have changed my mind?"

Peter didn't answer him. He put a few sticks below the kettle and the water sizzled.

Robert got down on his knees, pulled out his boots from below the table, and knocked them hard against the stone floor.

"Get the horse in the cart and I'll wet the tea . . . . . Will ye have a pair of eggs?"

"I won't have any eggs."

"And why won't you have an egg?"

"I don't want one, that's all."

Peter went out. When he came in again, Robert had bowls of tea on the table and two boiled eggs on Peter's plate. They supped the tea loudly and a contentment filled Robert when he saw Peter eating the eggs.

A hen came in through the open door, looked sideways at the table, and snatched a crust from the floor.

"Whisht on out o' that," Robert rattled his boots at it. "Ye'd think they never seen mate in their lives; it must be the sea air gives them the appetite."

Peter said nothing.

"I'll be back as soon as I can," Robert shouted from the cart. "What's this now the size of boots ye take?" And then he added quickly and in a sharper tone, "Weed a few drills to-day; that yellow weed will have the purties destroyed," and he looked at his growing potatoes and the yellow weed thick amongst them. Soon he turned his back to the sea and made inland; once he looked back and saw Peter standing against the gable.

It was late in the afternoon when he reached Downpatrick,

and it was sunset when he was ready to leave, a bag of yellow meal in the cart, a young lamb with its feet tied, bacon and candles, a few badly-tied parcels, and a pair of heavy boots for Peter. It was still bright but the rain was falling and, sitting in his cart, he sought shelter under a big chestnut tree. The heavy drops rattled down through the leaves and he pulled up the ears of his coat and threw an empty sack over the young lamb. He hated the long journey before him and recalled the day they had brought Peter along the same road and how Alice had pinned her shawl about his shoulders. "God be good to her but she was the kindly craythure!"

The rain slackened and he moved off. He felt cold. Steam arose from the horse's back and rain water lay near the tail-board, straw floating on it. The brown paper parcels were sodden. He shut his eyes and dozed.

The headlights of a motor wakened him and he drew the horse to the side and lit the lamp. The cart jolted in the puddles on the road. He shrugged his shoulders. He'd soon be home; the fire would be reddened for him, the kettle on the boil, and the lamp in the window. He urged on the horse and presently came within the sound of the sea. The waves rolled in slowly and broke with a tired splash. . . . . .

Peter leaned over the rail of the boat that was taking him to Liverpool. It was dark and cold, the deck wet, and all the passengers gone below except himself and an old seaman who walked quietly up and down. Out from the ship's side the waves swirled white and beyond them was darkness, and beyond that again lighthouse beams swept the sky.

Peter hailed the seaman: "Could you tell me where Strang-ford Lough would lie?"

The seaman stood beside him. "There's the Copeland Light aft and there's St. John's Lighthouse; midway between them would be Strangford — a treacherous lough!" and he paced the deck again.

Peter peered into the darkness towards a land that he could not see.

Flocks of thoughts crowded his mind; the lobsters and the fishing . . . . . the cow on the road . . . . the corn growing in the fields . . . . . the reading about the locusts . . . . . and the death of Alice . . . . .

A cold sorrow swept over him and tears formed in his eyes. He gripped the iron-rail and tried to stifle his grief.

Below someone laughed, a door opened, and a thick smell of tobacco floated out to him. And he thought of Robert jolting home in the cart to a hearth cold for his return. He shuddered. A piercing sense of utter worthlessness crept into his soul, the tears flowed thickly down his cheeks, and he could no longer see the lighthouse beams that wavered across the land.

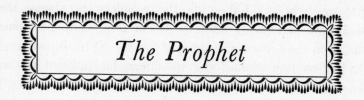

The Prophet

BRENDAN stood on the big stone near the byre, letting the rain splash on his bare head and dribble down his face. It was cold standing barefooted on the stone, but he didn't seem to mind, for now and again he'd stick out his tongue to catch the tickling drops. The byre door was open and the dark entrance showed the rain falling in grey streaks; it stuttered in the causeway and trickled in a puddle around the stone carrying with it bits of straw and hens' feathers. Beside him was a steaming manure heap with a pitchfork sticking in the top, its handle varnished with the rain. Under a heeled-up cart stood hens, humped and bedraggled, their grey eyelids blinking slowly with sleep.

Brendan shouted at them and laughed at the way they stretched their necks and shook the rain off their feathers. He waited until they hunched again to sleep and then he let another yell followed by louder laughs. A white duck clattering from behind the byre caught his attention. It stopped, looking from side to side, then it flapped its wings and quacked loudly. Brendan thought this was a sign for the rain to stop and he clodded the duck with few lumps of turf. He looked up at the sky and out to sea. The sky was grey: the Mull of Kintyre was smothered in fog; and turning round he saw a tonsure of mist on Knocklayde. He smiled at the prospect of more rain.

Presently, a latch clicked and his mother flung out a basin of water which splashed on the cobbles, the sleepy hens awakening and racing towards it. For a moment the woman leaned on the half-door, looking at her son, at his brown jersey black with rain around the shoulders, his tattered trousers clinging to his wet-pink knees, and his bare legs streaked with mud.

"Brendan, boy!" she shouted. "What in under Heaven are ye doin' there? Come in out o' that this minute or ye'll be foundered."

Brendan hopped off the stone, and as he entered the house he ducked when his mother made a clout at him. Inside he stood near the hearth with the steam rising from off his clothes and the rain trickling darkly on the stone floor.

"Dry yerself with that cloth, you silly boy: do ye want to go like yer Granda?"

Brendan didn't speak; he sat down on a stool near the fire, rubbing his head with the cloth, and thinking of Granda — poor Granda that died last month! If his mother only knew, it was like Granda he wanted to be; not to be dead, but to be able to tell the weather. His Granda could always tell when it was going to rain or snow.

Brendan pictured him sitting at the corner of the hearth, leaning forward on his stick, and the red handkerchief with the white spots sticking out of his pocket. He saw his brown beard and moustache, and the dark toothless mouth that reminded him of a thrush's nest. In his mind he heard his Granda groaning and saying: "There's bad weather in it, Brendan me son; there's bad weather coming for I feel it in my bones."

"And how do you feel it, Granda?" Brendan would ask.

"When you're old like me, me son, it's maybe you'll feel it

too, but God grant you won't. Standin' out on the mountainside
with the sheep and it rainin' heaven's hard, and you without
another coat to your back. And out at the fishin' at night with
the cold wind and the frozen lines, and your trousers clammed
to your knees. Your boots squelchin' in the shughs after divils
of cows, and may be not a bite of shop's meat from one year to
another. In water and out of water, in shughs and out of shughs;
'tis them things, Brendan, that'd make you feel it; 'tis them
things . . . . . ."

"Under Heaven, Brendan," shouted his mother interrupting
his thoughts, "you're scorchin'!"

Brendan became aware of the biscuity smell of scorched
clothes and felt his damp legs and knees sticky with heat. He
still held the cloth in his hand.

"Gimme that," said his mother, taking the cloth and vigorously rubbing his head. "Get up to bed now for ye have me
heart scalded this blessed day."

Brendan asked for a piece of bread and went up to the room
off the kitchen. His younger brother Bob was already asleep.
Brendan stood at the little four-paned window, eating his piece,
and looking out. He could hear the Lighthouse rockets shatter-
ing the rain-cold air and he knew the mists were thickening on
land and sea. It was getting dark. The hens had left the shelter
of the cart and gone to roost, the manure heap still steamed,
and Prince, the sheep-dog, nosed around the byre with soaking
paws and his hairy tail corded with rain. Brendan wondered
could Prince tell the weather for he was always in water and
out of water, in shughs and out of shughs.

He turned from the window and knelt on the bare, boarded
floor to say his prayers. He prayed to his Granda to help him
to tell the weather, and his mind wandered to the school and to

the boys asking him what kind of a day will it be to-morrow. He glowed at the thought and snuggled in beside his warm brother. He put his cold feet on his back and Bob wakened and threatened to shout to Mammie if he wouldn't lie over.

"All right," said Brendan. "I was going to tell you how to tell the weather, but I'll not do it now."

"Ach, no one could tell the weather only Granda," replied Bob sleepily.

"Couldn't they? Granda told me the secret and I can tell it."

Bob didn't reply and tried to sleep again. But Brendan lay awake and thought he felt something, felt his shoulders cold, and wondered if that's what Granda felt.

"Bob," he said, putting his cold feet on his brother again, "there's goin' to be rain to-morrow."

Bob heard him, but didn't speak, and soon the two boys fell asleep.

In the morning they set off for school, Brendan taking his little brother by the hand. It wasn't raining, but the air was cold and damp. The sky was grey like the evening before, and water lay in the cart-ruts along the road. Below them the sea lay calm with dark paths zig-zagging across it, while the hills around were sodden and beaten into cold, shrivelled shapes. As their bare feet slapped the wet road, Brendan kept telling his brother how he had foretold the weather, and little Bob listened with great belief and pride. Now and again they'd stop and look at the imprint of bare feet on the rain-softened road trying to guess what boy had passed along before them.

When they got into the one-roomed school there was an air of restless gaiety, for to-morrow was to be the School Sports. Bob was full of his big brother's magic, and began telling everyone how his Brendan could tell the weather. Then one little boy put up his hand saying, "Sir! Sir! he says his brother can tell the weather."

The master looked over at Brendan whose toes were twitching under the desk.

"Can you forecast the weather?" asked the master. Brendan's face got red and the master smiled. "I never knew we had a prophet in the school before. And what kind of a day will it be to-morrow?" he added. But Brendan never spoke.

On account of the Sports the school was let out early, the scholars gushing from the door in all directions. Brendan and Bob were not alone now. The three Lighthouse boys were with them chaffing about the weather.

"What'll it be like for the Sports?" says one. "Oh, Prophet of Israel," says another, imitating the master's voice, "what will there be to-morrow?" Brendan walked on in silence and they laughed and chanted;

> "Oh, the prophet!
> The prophet!
> The rick-stick-stophet!"

Then Brendan stopped, and felt, felt something. "I'll tell ye — " he says, "if ye want to know. There'll be rain to-morrow, bucketfuls and bucketfuls of it."

"And how do you know?" they all said together.

"It's me Granda that learned me before he died."

A great silence came on them.

"Tell me how to do it and I'll give you a puffin's egg and I'll show you me robin's nest," asked one earnestly. Brendan didn't answer and they walked beside him, looking at him as if he were a black man.

He turned into the house and his companions walked on for a while in silence.

"I bet you a million pounds he can't tell the weather," ventured one.

"You're right," said another, "for doesn't Father McKinley get us to pray for a good day when the Bishop is comin' for Confirmation."

"We'll see to-morrow anyhow; but mind you his Granda was a quare ould fella and me Da often said he was an ould witch," replied the eldest.

From the kitchen window Brendan watched his three companions disappear down the road and he knew that they were talking about him. He clenched his fists and wished with all his might for rain to-morrow, while his Granda's words, like an old rhyme, ran through his mind — "in water and out of water, in shughs and out of shughs, 'tis them things that make you feel it!"

After the dinner he went off with Bob to the lake to sail boats. Brendan's was a Norwegian schooner, a flat, pointed stick with two big goose feathers. A nail with a piece of cord was stuck in her stern so that she could tow Bob's little, one-masted vessel. Brendan watched his boat crinkling the water, leaving a trail behind it like a swimming duck. With his trousers rolled up he waded out as far as he could go, following his boat and chanting — "in water and out of water, in shughs and out of shughs."

Coming home he was wet to the skin, but there was great joy in his heart for he felt now there'd be rain to-morrow.

That night he prayed for a long time, prayed to God and to his Granda to bring on the rain, and in bed he thought he felt whatever Granda felt. At one time he was sure he felt the rain

at the window, but it was only the fuchsia leaves brushing against the pane. He lay for awhile thinking of wet days with the rain sizzling in the lake, the hens hunched up under the cart, the ducks suttering in the shughs, and Prince running across the kitchen floor with wet paws. And from such thoughts sleep came.

In the morning he awoke and lay listening, listening for the sound of rain. But outside the birds sang and in the window a large fly buzzed. He raised himself on his elbows and stared around. A blue sky was framed in the window. The sun was shining and a leafy shadow of the fuchsia bush trembled on the white-washed bedroom wall. The birds' songs came clearer now to his keener wakefulness. He looked at his sleeping brother. Then he lay back on the pillow, and dripping drearily into his mind came thoughts of his companions jeering and shouting — *The Prophet! The Prophet!*

The Schooner

I T WAS August and very warm; Terence Devlin, a boy of
eight, was leaving the city with his father for a holiday on
the Island of Rathlin. It was early morning when they walked
to the station where porters were rim-rolling milk cans along
the empty platform. At Ballymoney they had to change and
wait for a long time for the narrow-gauge train to take them to
Ballycastle. That train was very small and the people seemed
too big for it; steam dribbled from all parts of the engine and
Terence held on tightly to his father for he feared that it would
explode at any moment. The wooden seats in the carriage were
rough and hacked with names, and they hurt the backs of his
knees. In the floor boards there were wide slits and through
them could be seen the sharp stones which lay between the
sleepers. The train shook violently and Terence's teeth rattled
in his head and the suitcase fell off the rack on to the floor.

"I hope you'll not be sea-sick in the train," his father smiled
to him, and put away the paper he was trying to read. When
the train slowed down he would shout out to his son the names
of flowers and mosses that grew on the rocky embankments.
But to amuse himself Terence dropped cigarette-cards between
the floor boards and spelt out words that were pencilled on the
ceiling. His father told him to try and sleep and not be strain-
ing his eyes reading words that were written by bad boys: "It's

the like of those things that bring a bad name on the country. I hope, Terence, you'll never scribble in a railway carriage."

After that Terence dozed off and when he awoke he was in Ballycastle. There was the smell of turf and the air was heavy with heat. Down past a siding they walked where the wooden sleepers were sticky with oil and smelt sharply of tar.

They stopped at a shop and Terence bought ice-cream, a wooden spade, and a red bucket with black letters: *A Present from Ballycastle*.

They took the long road to the sea. Men with twisted towels round their necks passed them. Blinds were pulled down in the big houses and on the lawns old ladies sat on deck-chairs under the shade of red umbrellas. Terence shook a pebble from his sandal, and Mr. Devlin walked on, fanning himself with his hat. The big chestnut trees that lined the road were stiff with heat, but under the leaves flakes of shadow quivered. The tarred road crackled as a motor raced by, then a drove of cattle came up, their hooves sticking in the tar, their dung-caked sides as dry as the bark of a tree.

"If we get weather like this, Terence, we'll not know ourselves on the way back."

While Mr. Devlin went to inquire about the boat Terence leaned over a sun-warmed wall and saw below him boys and girls playing tennis. Boys hung blazers on the net-posts, hitched up their belts, and through the sun-sifted air came the cord-rattle of tennis balls hitting the net and nearby a lazy plunge of waves falling on a curve of sand. Idly he picked moss out of the crevices in the wall, and then a finger flicked his ear and he turned to see his father smiling down at him: 'We'll go over to the quay now, the boat's going to the island shortly."

Alongside the quay lay a boat, a brown sail wrapped round

the mast and old motor tyres hanging over the sides. The out-
going tide had left pools of water on the quay, and strands
of seaweed had entangled themselves under the mooring rings.
At the end of the quay three boys were fishing for fry and
behind them sat glass jamjars filled with shining water and
green moss. Terence yearned to take off his sandals and
dabble his scorched feet in the pools, but already his father
was handing the suit-case to a man in the boat and he joined
him to see the cargo being taken aboard: two bags of flour,
a tea-chest filled with loaves and covered with sacking, a coil
of barbed wire and two panes of glass.

There were five islanders, some tall and awkward-looking,
standing loosely as if they were ashamed of their height. Terence and his father sat in the stern; the tyres were pulled in,
and one of the crew lifted an oar and pushed the boat out from
the quay. The gunwale was warm and blobs of resin had oozed
out of the wood. The sky was clear, the sea smooth and a fierce
sun striking in to it.

Ballast stones were dropped overboard and Terence saw the
water fizzle white and felt splashes of salt on his lips. Four
oars were fixed between the thole-pins and dipped into the
water simultaneously; drops dripped from the blades, whorls
were left by the thrust of the oars, and looking back Terence
watched for a long time the wrinkled patches of water fade
into the smooth sea. He could still hear the dull thud of waves
on the sand and he wondered in what part of the ocean the
waves were hatched. He was going to ask his father, but he
was now pointing out Fair Head to him and telling him a story
about beautiful children who had been turned into swans and
how for many lonely years they had wandered about this sea.

Far out from the Head two steamers were very black and

seemed to float in the sky. Gulls flew close to the boat, their reflections clear in the smooth water; puffins stood up and flapped their wings, or to escape the boat they arose in a flock and flittered the top of the water with their feet. But for all the rowing the island seemed to draw no nearer. It lay spread out in front of them, its white cliffs like a row of teeth, and to the right its black cliffs polished by the sun.

"Now, men," said Mr. Devlin, "I could give one of you a spell," and he took an oar, splashed awkwardly, and broke the rhythmic dip-and-lift which had fascinated Terence.

"Don't dip the blade so deep," said one of the islanders, and with great patience he showed Mr. Devlin how to feather his oar. In no time the sweat was gleaming on Mr. Devlin's forehead, and soon he had to take off his coat and waistcoat.

"It's tough work when yer not used to it," said a little brown-faced man who was rowing near the bow.

Mr. Devlin grunted and turned around to look at the island: "I'm damned if we're moving at all. I thought we'd row over in ten minutes."

"No, nor in ten times ten minutes. 'Tis a long pull — eight miles across."

Mr. Devlin puffed loudly and his oar left no whirling holes in the water. Presently he gave up: "Gentlemen, I think I've worked my passage," and he sat in the stern and his hands fell limply on his lap.

Later Mr. Devlin began to ask questions about the island, and the boatmen answered him, and in his own mind he began to plan what walks he would take during his fortnight's holiday. Terence picked out the white houses that lay in the scoops of the hills and the square-towered church and graveyard that edged the coast. Now the boat was passing between two

quays, and a clump of men with their hands in their pockets
gazed at the boat as she came in. There was a strong smell of
rotting seaweed rising from the bay. White ducks were dozing
on the grass above tide-mark; along the strand a man in his
shirt-sleeves was carrying two cans of water, and a barefooted
boy was throwing a stick into the water for a black dog to
retrieve it.

Terence and his father made their way up the stony quay,
past a rusty winch and a broken boat with green-scummed
water. The houses were low and slated, and one of them with
two sentry-box porches had its name in Gaelic letters printed
on a thin board.

"This is our ticket," said Mr. Devlin, and they walked up a
gravel path towards it.

A tall woman in black opened the door: "Welcome to the
island," she said. "We didn't see the boat comin' in or faith we'd
have sent Paddy down to meet it. . . . Come on in. Annie's
bakin' and the place is a bit throughother."

They were in a warm kitchen with a shining range, and
Annie was turning farls of bread on a griddle and hurried to
greet them: "Ye must be famished with the hunger. I'll not be
long gettin' the things on the table."

The two women were dressed alike: black blouses with high
collars, grey hair topped with big combs, but Annie had on a
spotted apron, and two broad rings were grooved so tightly on
her finger that the flesh was swollen at each side.

"Lizzie," she said quietly, "take their things up to the room,"
and she stood beside Terence, holding his cap and stroking
his fair hair.

A door opened on the opposite side of the kitchen and Paddy
slouched in, his sleeves rolled up, a rough-haired terrier at his

heels. The dog began to bark at the strangers and Paddy swiped at him with his hat: "Chu, you brute! Chu, Bumper, and have some manners!"

He shook hands with Terence and Mr. Devlin, and then sat beside them on the sofa, idly picking clay from his fingers with his thumb nail. Annie moved from the table to the griddle: she was very quiet, shadow-like, her elastic-sided boots making no noise, her eyes withdrawn and brooding.

The kitchen was big: a wag-at-the-wall ticked loudly, and in the deep window that faced the sea there was a white spool, a yellow tape, and a calendar with its leaves curled and a red outline of a fish on all the Friday dates.

"Ye got a lovely day for crossin', so ye did," put in Paddy. "It was a long pull, but ye had the tide with ye."

"There wasn't a ripple. I never saw the sea so calm," answered Mr. Devlin.

Annie scraped the griddle noisily with a knife and swept the scrapings in to her hand with a goose's wing. Paddy crossed and re-crossed his legs.

"The sea was like oil," continued Mr. Devlin, trying to make conversation. "And it was covered with birds."

Annie dropped the knife, and then quietly opened the back door and went out.

Paddy got to his feet, glancing at the door: "Calm weather is scarce in these parts. There wasn't an air of wind the past two days." He stuffed a piece of twisted paper between the bars of the grate and lit his pipe. "Weather like this would do no good; the soil's as dry as snuff."

Annie came in and Paddy added hurriedly: "And, Mr. Devlin, while you're here you must get a night or two's fishin'. The sea's thick with fish." He hitched his belt: "I'll leave ye now till ye get your tay. I've a field of purties I have to weed."

Bumper slid out from under the table, but when he saw Lizzie enter with an old raincoat he wagged his tail.

Lizzie smiled at Terence and turned to the dog: "Bumper, are ye goin' to Ballycarry?" The dog jumped into the air three times, ran under the stairs and came out with a basket in his mouth.

Terence laughed and said to his father: "Could I go to Ballycarry?"

Lizzie folded her arms: "Ah, child, it's too far. It's away up in the mountains, but if you come here next year you'll be a big boy and I'll take you and Bumper up to Ballycarry."

Kneeling on the sofa he watched through the window: Bumper walked in front, the basket in his mouth; Lizzie followed, a gleaming can hooked to her elbow. They passed behind a limestone wall, her head bobbing up and down; then the road swept alongside a hill, dipped into a hollow and they were lost from sight.

For the next two days while his father tramped the island gathering specimens of wildflowers Terence played about the house waiting for the time when Bumper and Lizzie were to set out for Ballycarry. On the third day he was strolling about like that when he saw the door of a little lean-to lying open. Cautiously he went in and found Annie sharpening a knife on a hone. She didn't hear him. The sun was shining through a small window and the shadow of a bush flickered against the pane. It was cool and quiet, and broken cobwebs dangled from the bare slates. There was no sound except the rasp of the knife. He was going to go out when he saw on a shelf a model schooner with brown sails, brass hooks and rings, and underneath the tail-shaped stern the painted name: *Windswept*.

"Oh," he said, "who owns the lovely boat?"

Annie started at the voice and turning round she saw him tapping the deck and moving the sails backwards and forwards. Silently she stared at him. He stroked the hull with the palm of his hand and toyed with the helm.

"Who owns it?" he asked again, his eyes wide with anticipated joy.

For a moment she was rigid, then she relaxed, and a look of brooding doubt spread across her face. Again he tapped the deck, and her expression changed to one of patient sadness.

"You can play with it," she said, almost in a whisper. "You can play with it, and Paddy will show you how to trim the sails."

In a minute he was out and off to the shore. Paddy met him: "Where are you goin' with that! You can't have that!" he said in great surprise.

"Annie lent it to me. She said I could play with it and you could fix the sails for me."

"Wait now a minute. Don't go away." And Paddy hurried up to the little lean-to. Annie was standing in the shadow of the doorway and came to meet him. Both raised their hands and waved to Terence to go on. Paddy followed him, thinking how long the little schooner had remained on its stand and how for many years Annie had polished it: "It's curious the changes that come over people — changes ye'd never dream of." And he rubbed the back of his neck with his hand.

He sat on the beach stones above the little bay, took the schooner on his lap and showed Terence how to use the helm: "Turn it to the left when you're sailin' her with her bow pointin' to the house."

Terence took off his sandals and placed the schooner in the water. All her sails tightened in the breeze and her brass rings glinted in the sun. Annie saw it from the door: the rust-brown sails, the wet-gleaming hull, and the silver flakes of water skimming from the bow. Paddy walked along the strand, then a disturbing thought whorled in his mind, for he wondered was the ship watertight after her years on the stand. He called to Terence to bring it up to him, and with his ear to the hull he turned the boat up and down; he could hear nothing except a slight seed-rattle of a chip of wood inside her.

"She's as tight as a pig-skin — a lovely boat! She's the girl can whip along in a thin breeze . . . Take good care of her."

All that day Terence played with the boat, and in the evening after his supper Annie, with a thin shawl on her shoulders came down to the shore to bring him home. The sun had gone down and the water was darkened by a chilly breeze.

He shouted: "Look now!" as the boat tore across the bay and a knife-curve of water rolled white at her bow.

"Come, Terence, it's gettin' late. What'll your father say if you're not in bed when he comes back from fishin'."

She waited on the shore road for him, and presently he came floundering up the loose stones of the beach with the schooner hugged to his breast. He was out of breath and full of joy. Then he saw that her eyes were wet.

"What's wrong?" he asked.

"I was just thinkin'," she answered clumsily and tried to draw his attention to a shower of moths that flickered over a field of beans.

"But why were you crying?" he persisted.

"I was thinking of the boat. It was my husband made it."

"And will he make one for me?" Terence asked eagerly.

"Indeed, he'd make you one."

"And when will he make it? Where is he?" he kept repeating. "Where is he?"

She stood still on the road: "When he comes back, please God, he'll make you one."

"And when will he be back?"

"It's getting cold. We must hurry now," she evaded.

There was great heat in the kitchen from the humming range. The curtains were drawn and the oil lamp lighted. Terence was allowed to look at the book of flowers that his father had already gathered and sometimes Annie would bend over him, take from her apron pocket a sugar lump, and put it in his mouth. He loved this time of the evening with no one in the kitchen but the two of them, and even Annie, herself, looked forward to this hour before his bedtime. He was great company. Sometimes he would thread her needle and she would sit and watch him, her hands loosely on her lap. She would give him milk to drink and he would sit near the range feeling the heat on his knees and hearing outside the unhurried breath of the waves. Then when he would nod his head in sleep she would light a candle and bring him to his room. She used to allow him to keep the schooner under the dressing table, but one evening when she heard him coughing she stole upstairs and found him asleep on the floor beside the schooner.

The next day she feared he would have a cold, but he set off with his father to swim and later she coaxed him to sit with her in the sunny field at the back of the house. The foot of the field had a crop of blossomed potatoes and Paddy was spraying them with blue stone and from where they sat they could hear the spray rattling like hail on the leaves and see the blue sheen of it as it dried in the sun. Butterflies pirouetted over the field and Terence caught one and placed it on the palm of his hand. The powder from its wings clung to his fingers and he put the butterfly on the ground and it began to struggle up a blade of grass.

"It'll never fly again," Annie said to him as she looked over the calm sea. "The powder on its wings means as much to it as wind for the sails of a boat."

The remark hurt him and he watched with growing sorrow the blade of grass bending under the weight of the ungainly butterfly and how brilliantly white its helpless wings shone in the sun.

Paddy came up to them for a drink from the can of milk, his eyebrows and clothes covered with a fine blue dust. One foot crushed the butterfly, and Terence was going to cry out when he noticed that Annie was engrossed in her knitting and didn't see what had happened. Presently she got up and went inside to get ready the tea, leaving her rug and knitting in the field.

"Do you know what you've done?" said Terence to Paddy. "You've tramped on a butterfly and killed it."

"And sure what sin is there in that," replied Paddy, noticing how his lips quivered. "Sure they only live for a day and some of them don't live as long as that — the swallows and thrushes snap them in two while you'd wink."

Paddy lay back and pulled his hat over his face. Terence took off his sandals and felt the soft grass on his bare feet. He closed his eyes from the glare of the sun and thoughts of cool things stirred within his mind — moss floating in a jamjar, drops on the blade of an oar, and rain washing the powder from a butterfly's wings. He sat up and on gazing at the sea he saw that a schooner with all her canvas out was passing up the sound.

"Oh, Paddy, look at the lovely schooner like Annie's!"

Paddy took the hat from his eyes and stared at the ship: "It's not often you see them about now. They're a grand sight. That one is only drifting up there on the first of flood -- there's no wind for her."

"I'll run and tell Annie."

"Come back here and let her make the tay," and he rose to his feet. "Come on with me and spray the spuds."

Terence hesitated: "Let me tell her!"

"You'll not!" Paddy said sharply. "Do what I say!"

Reluctantly Terence came over to him, and slowly they walked down to the barrel of spray, Paddy looking now and again at the schooner and calculating how long it would take her to drift out of the sound, knowing also that she would surely drift back again if the wind did not rise during the night.

He got Terence to pick up the flinty pieces of limestone that lay between the drills and to search under all the leaves for the Queen of the butterflies. "And you'll know her," says Paddy, "by her wings, for she has one wing of pure gold and one of shining silver, and if you find her you'll be able to sell her for hundreds of pounds." And while Terence searched, Paddy sprayed until the schooner had nearly passed up the sound. Then clapping the dust from his hands he went to the top of the field and gathered up the rug and the knitting.

When they came in Lizzie and Bumper had arrived from Ballycarry, and Bumper lay at the open door in the sun snapping at the flies. The cement floor was cold under Terence's feet and Annie made him sit down at once and put on his sandals.

As the evening grew old the warmth left the earth and the potato-blossoms closed up and drooped their heads. In the kitchen a warm silence crept into all the corners and a trapped fly buzzed madly in a web.

During the night a rainy storm blew against the house, and in the morning when Terence wakened he saw his father standing at the window: "Terence, boy, it's like a winter's morning. The summer's finished and to-morrow, if the boat can leave, you'll be on your way back again."

Two conflicting thoughts encumbered the boy's mind: a desire that the storm would last a long time so that no boat could leave; a desire that the storm would die at once so that he could get sailing the schooner before he left. At breakfast he heard Paddy assure his father that the storm would last no time and that it would blow itself out before night.

When Annie was making the beds Terence went with her and from the window they looked out upon the bay. Ducks and hens sheltered under the boats that were hauled up on the grass. The wind flayed the water into jagged peaks; waves tore between the two quays, crashed on the strand, and sent jabbling fingers amongst the stones on the beach. Gulls rose from the stones and tipped the waves before they broke. Tangles of brown sea-wrack curved the bay and clumps of it floated in a stolid mass.

"Oh, look!" Terence would call out as a big wave struck the quay and burst in snowy spray. Annie would cross to the window and share for a moment the vigorous joy of wind-torn water.

When she had the beds made Terence shyly plucked her apron: "Could I have the boat?"

"Terry, you have no sense — one wave would smash the

riggin' and leave it like a butterfly that had lost its wings," and she stroked his head and smiled at him meekly.

"Well, could I have it after awhile if the wind goes away?"

"We'll see."

In the afternoon the wind had fallen, and late that evening when the wind was exhausted and only a glimmer of it flicked across the bay Terence pleaded again for the boat.

Annie laughed at him: "At this time! Ye'd be frozen down on the shore."

"Ah, please, I'll be going away in the morning."

"But sure you'll be back next year and you can sail it till your heart's content."

"Just one more for the last," he kept pleading.

Paddy was dozing on the sofa, and Lizzie was trying to read a paper in the light from the fire, but did not raise her head.

Terence asked again.

"All right," said Annie, and getting the key she went out for the schooner. "Just sail her once. Darkness will soon be here."

The chilly water took his breath away as he set the rudder and let the boat slide from his hand. As he ran along the cold strand he could see the sails black against the light from the water. He sailed her back across the bay again and then heard Annie call to him from the lighted doorway.

"I'm going now," he shouted, waiting for the boat to come to shore. But then something happened. The schooner stopped, tangled in a clump of floating wrack. He waited for her to free herself. Then he noticed she was slewing round. He clenched his hands and involuntarily pressed his feet into the sand. The sails flapped, caught the wind, and she headed out between the two quays towards the open sea. He began to cry. He ran to the first quay. He skinned his legs as he climbed on to it from the strand. Annie called to him again, but he didn't hear her. He lifted a boat-hook that lay on the quay and peered at the waves that slopped in amongst the stone-steps. Once he thought he saw something pass at great speed, but he wasn't sure. Backwards and forwards he ran from one quay to the other like a dog that had lost his master. Desperately he searched, lifting up sand-soaked tins and flinging them into the water. His throat was scorched. He heard Annie call to him from the shore: "Terence, Terence, are you there?"

He went back to look for his sandals. The incoming tide had almost covered them. Annie came down to him over the beach stones: "Where did you get to?"

He couldn't answer. When she came close to him she saw him without the boat and heard him sobbing.

"Where's the boat?" she asked.

Through his tears he told her how he had fixed the rudder and how the boat had caught in wrack and had turned round. She stood beside him and squeezed his head against her breast: "Don't cry, Terence. Don't take it so ill." A deep shivering convulsed her and she squeezed him with great possessiveness and stroked his hair.

Paddy and Lizzie were seated at the fire and looked questioningly at Annie when they saw Terence's scratched legs and the tears in his eyes.

"He lost the boat," said Annie, "and he's broken-hearted." An awkward silence fell. Lizzie poked the fire and Paddy fumbled in his pockets.

"Wash your face and legs and don't let your father see you in that state," and she made much noise under the stairs getting a basin and a towel. Lizzie and Paddy said nothing.

"Don't cry; sure that could happen to anyone?" she said, drying his face and legs.

"It was the rudder. . . . I fixed it right and it caught in sea weed on the way over and turned round."

"They're a misfortunate thing to put on any model boat," put in Paddy.

Annie stared at him, and he went out and walked about until the lamp had been lowered in the kitchen and all had gone to bed.

In the morning it was raining heavily and some sheep that were to be taken to the mainland stood on the quay bleating and calling to others that were being driven along the strand. Dogs were barking, and drenched men with no overcoats shouted to one another. Mr. Devlin heard them as he washed, and he hurried Terence out of bed and carried down the suitcase to the kitchen.

"There'll be a bit of a jabble on the sea," said Paddy as they sat down to their breakfast. "It's raining badly and I have an ould bit of a sail you can spread on your knees."

He looked out of the door: "Yiv plenty of time — eat yer fill. They're carrying the sheep to the boat but I'll not bring my three down till yer nearly ready."

Through the open door they could hear the melancholy bleat of sheep and see a loose web of rain wind-trailed across the bay.

Annie was quiet: "You'll send Terence back next year for all his holidays. Paddy, there, could meet the train at Ballycastle."

"Would you like that?" said Mr. Devlin.

Terence nodded his head. He wanted to talk about the

schooner, but he knew if he opened his mouth no words would come.

Paddy carried the suit-case to the boat, Lizzie and Bumper followed. In the porch Annie held Terence's hand: "It won't be long till next summer and if God spares us all you'll be back again."

He couldn't look up at her and he noticed that stains of salt water had whitened the toes of his sandals.

"Good-bye," she said and watched them go down the gravel path.

They clambered into the wet-soaked boat and a man rubbed a seat for them with a wisp of straw. When Paddy had tied the legs of his sheep he carried them aboard and sat beside Terence and Mr. Devlin. The sail was unrolled from the mast and blobs of rain-water fell from its folds; it filled in the breeze and the driving rain rattled on it like countless bird-pecks. Lizzie stood on the quay with her arms folded and Bumper ran around shaking the rain from himself. From the porch Annie waved to Terence; the tears came to his eyes and he pretended to look for something under the seat. The water slid past the boat, her bows crunched into the waves, and Terence raised his head and scanned the shore for the schooner. But he could see nothing, only black rocks with waves jumping over them. Slanting clouds heaved up against the hills and stitched the valleys with rain. The houses were falling behind and soon there would be nothing to mark them except the big telegraph pole above the post-office.

The wet sheep lay on yellow straw, steam was rising from them, and now and again with the pitch of the boat they tried to scramble to their feet. The rain wormed down the bit of sail that was spread across Terence's knees, and Paddy tried to light his pipe by pulling the edge of the sail over his head.

Terence now searched the sea, and his gaze was so prolonged and intense that Mr. Devlin nudged Paddy: "He's looking for the boat."

"Ach, God knows where she is by this time," replied Paddy.

"Would it cost much to replace it ?"

"Ach, Mr. Devlin, it's not the cost that matters — it's what it meant to Annie," and he bent confidentially to Mr. Devlin. "It was her husband that made it thirty years ago. It was a model of his own ship and since he went away she cleaned and polished it. It held raw memories for her!"

"Where is he now?" Mr. Devlin asked.

"He never came back. They were married in June and early in September of the same year he went away and she never saw him again."

"Were they . . . happy?"

"Happy! . . . He was a ship's carpenter — a fine lump of a fella — and made every stick of furniture that went into their house. They lived at Ballycarry on the East side of the island. We still have the house, but she never goes there now. . . . She still thinks he'll come back."

"And will he, do you think?"

Paddy shook his head: "He'll not, poor fella. I think he's drowned."

Terence's eyes were on the sea, but sometimes when a sheep would move he would stretch out his hand and pat its wet head. Paddy spoke in a low voice, but Terence wasn't listening to him.

"They spent three happy months together on the island," continued Paddy. "His ship was bound for Canada for a load of grain. It left the Clyde and it was to pick him up passing the island. He was on the look-out for it and when it came into the sound they sent a small boat ashore for him. But at night the wind had fallen and the schooner was becalmed."

Mr. Devlin noticed that his suit-case was lying flat and the rain was creeping into it, but he did not move and inclined his head nearer to Paddy's.

"Annie kept her light in the window and at dawn she was down on the shore looking out at the great schooner. She waved, knowing he'd see her. The next day the ship was still there. It was a day like the one you met coming to the island — terribly warm. But during the night a wind sprung up and she saw her lights moving out of the sound. . . . That was the last she saw."

"And what happened?"

"The boat nor crew were never heard tell of. . . . She always felt that he was alive and that he'd come back. . . . She's got very old waiting. . . . For awhile she used to walk about the house at night, opening and shutting doors. But she got over that."

"It's a great pity Terence lost the little schooner on her. She shouldn't have lent it to him."

"Ah, Mr. Devlin, she has great liking for your son — great liking. And you'll have to send him back next summer. The loss of the wee schooner may do good, for it's gone now and she won't be cleaning it and thinking. . . . There was times I wish somebody had stolen it."

They were both silent. Three big waves hit the boat and sent the spray flying over them.

"Man, Terence," said Paddy, "if the wee schooner met fellas like that they'd make short work of her. But, maybe, she's ashore somewhere below the white rocks."

"And will you look for her?"

"I will, I will," said Paddy, trying to relight his damp pipe. But the abstracted way he answered made Terence feel that the schooner meant nothing to Paddy; he knew he would never see it again and that he'd have no schooner to play with when he'd come back next year.

The Mother

SHE was seated at the parlour window in a blue frock, a gilt bangle on her wrist, and a copy of *Woman's Notes* open on her lap. Her attention was not given to the book, for she was watching the people passing in the street and the last of the autumn sun mellowing the small red-bricked houses opposite. Behind her in the hall her two little boys were playing and to their play she was giving no ear. Everyone that passed the window would glance at the fire blazing in the grate and then abruptly look away when they caught sight of the blue frock. She knew well what they'd be thinking. There she is, they would say, on the look-out for another husband and her other man not two years in his grave. And little cause she has to be marrying again, they'd add, and she with two nice little boys to keep her company and her widow's pension to keep her comfortable; and hadn't she her own father a while back with her, drawing his old-age pension and helping to keep the house respectable. But would they add that he smoked all his pension-money in his pipe? They would not. After all what did they really know about the inside of any house — nothing; nothing, except what their own evil natures would tell them.

Since she first came into the street she had made sure the neighbours wouldn't know much of her business. She had kept herself to herself, gave harm or hindrance to no one, and didn't join in the general borrowings of tea and sugar, and the running in and out of one another's houses. She had looked after her husband when he was alive, dressed her two boys neatly for school, saw them off in the morning, and instead of having a gossip with her next-door neighbour she would close the door, attend to her house and keep it clean in spite of the smuts from the factory chimneys that whorled down upon the street both day and night. But keeping herself to herself didn't please the neighbours. Too high in her ways she was. And hadn't they often shouted things at her little boys: "Run home now and tell that to your ladylike mother — her that was never seen with a thumb-mark of black-lead at the side of her nose. Her with her grand airs and graces and her face powdered and painted like a clown's in a circus — trying to look like twenty and she on the wrong side of forty." It wasn't once or twice they shouted that at her two innocent children. But did they ever remember the priest at the mission who began his sermon: "Is it wrong for a woman to paint her face?" and then took a handkerchief leisurely from his sleeve, blew his nose, and put the handkerchief back again. "No," he answered, "No, it is not wrong as long as she does it to attract a husband or to keep the one she has got." Very few of them, she was sure, remembered that. And this evening if Frank asked her would she marry again she would say yes — that'd let the neighbours see what she thought of them! She gave a laugh, half of joy and half of scorn, and *Woman's Notes* fell on to the oilclothed floor.

As she stooped to pick it up, she paused, listening to her two boys at play. She gripped the book and drew near to the open parlour door that led into the hall.

"You be granda now for awhile," John was saying to Tom.
"Lend me the stick then," Tom answered.

"No, no. Pretend you're him up in the workhouse — you're
best at that. Lie down on the mat like you done before."

Tom stretched out on the mat and pillowed his head on his
arms and began to imitate his granda: "'Tis terrible to be shut
up within four black walls and you without a friend in the
world. 'Tis terrible that you work hard all your life and this
is the end of it. Me that once wrought in the country and knew
the name of every bush and every tree. 'Tis terrible to be old
and be ordered away from your bit of fire, and now I am without spoon or cup to call my own. And I have to smoke at set
hours and have no little boys to chat with me of an evening."

"O, Tom, if granda heard you he'd laugh his eyes out, so
he would. Go on and give us more, Tom. Pretend you're talking to the man in the next bed. Begin: 'Are you asleep there,
Billdoe?' "

But Tom at that moment saw his mother standing her full
height in the doorway, and he sat up on the mat and stared at
her with a guilty, frightened look.

"Tom! John!" she said, the words husky in her throat. Her
breast heaved and she turned the bangle on her wrist. "Go
inside to the kitchen and I'll speak to you in a minute." There
was the sound of a lagging step in the street outside, and her
heart pounded in her ears, but the step passed on. She turned
into the parlour, and in the mirror above the mantelpiece
looked at her face and dabbed away the tears that had risen
to her eyes. She powdered her face, and rolling the magazine
in her hand went into the boys, now sitting in the dusk of the
kitchen.

Her voice was cold: "Where did I tell you your granda was.

Where?" she said to Tom. For a moment he didn't answer. She caught him by the arm: "Where have you to say your granda is? Do you hear me, Tom? Answer me — I'm not going to beat you."

"He's away to the country for the good of his health," Tom said.

"Say it again so that you'll not forget it. And you say it with him, John."

"He's away to the country for the good of his health," they said together.

"Don't let me ever hear you say anything else about him. If your granda was back at this fireside it wouldn't answer the two of you. It's not boots you'd have on your feet — you'd be running about barefoot like some of the other good-for-nothings in this locality." She rolled and unrolled the magazine as she spoke, and then some look in the younger's face reproached her and she put her arm round his shoulder and stroked his head: "Go on to bed now like good little boys. You've got your tea," and she stood and watched them climb the stairs.

"Shout down when you're in," she said. "And don't forget to say your prayers."

She went into the parlour again and took her seat at the window. The sun had set, and above the roof-tops a greenish light was tightly stretched across the sky. The lamplighter was passing up the street with his yellow pole over his shoulder, and a crowd of little girls scampered in front of him and held out their pinafores as they stood under a lamp awaiting the first pale blossom of light. Then as the pole was manoeuvred into the lamphead, the mantle lit with a plop, and they all shouted: "Silver and gold I hold in my lap," and ran ahead to the next lamp.

They should all be in bed, she thought, running mad about the streets to this time of night, and nobody to care about them whether they're hungry or whether they're dirty. She saw faces in the kitchen-windows opposite and the curtains pulled to the side to let in the last light of the day. She saw her own firelight reflected in the cold windowpane and the first stars appearing in the sky. The street was quiet now, and then a woman appeared in a doorway and called harshly: "Cissie, Jackie, where the hell are ye to this time o' night. Wait'll I lay my hands on ye!" There was a scurry of feet and a clash of doors. Darkness fell, and through the silence there was the rumble of machinery from the factory at the head of the street, a rumble that nobody noticed for it had become part and parcel of their lives as much as the ticking of a clock. But someday, please God, she'd get away from all this roughness, away to the fringes of the city where she'd have a house with an extra room, and, maybe, take her father out of the workhouse and bring him home again where he could sun himself in a patch of garden at the back and maybe see the whins in bloom on the mountain and hear the larks singing. "O God," she said aloud, "if one had to live one's life again!" Wasn't she always at Peter, when he was alive, to move away from this street and go to a place where the boys could get a corner of a field to kick football. But you couldn't move him! "The rent is cheap here," he always said. "The rent is cheap and what we save we'll put past for their education." It wasn't as if she hadn't thought about their education herself and how it would break her heart to see them astride a bicycle when they leave school and the name of some grocer painted in white on a big plate between the bars.

She sighed, rolled and unrolled the magazine on her lap, and glanced at the table set for two and the firelight glinting on the cups.

"We're in bed now, mother," Tom shouted from the room above the parlour.

She went up to them and sat on the bed and ran her fingers through their hair. "I'll tell you a secret and you musn't breathe it to anyone," she whispered. "It's a secret, mind you, and you musn't mention it to a living soul. Some day you'll have your granda back. And you'll have fields to play in and a real ball to kick on the grass, and never again will you be kicking a rag-ball between the lampposts in the street and have the neighbours complaining about you breaking their windows and tormenting their babies out of their sleep. It'll be a great day for us the day we bring your granda back."

"And will it come soon," they asked and laughed with nervous expectancy.

"It'll come soon, please God, and you'll see the fine house we'll have with three bedrooms. Not like this one with only two, and maybe we'll afford one with a bath in it. But, whatever comes, there'll be a bit of grass at the back where you can play ball."

"Can we get a dog?" John asked.

"I'll get you a dog. And maybe you'll have a new father that will make things for you and make a box for your dog."

"Where'll the house be?"

"It'll not be far away."

"How far?"

"It's a secret. Go asleep now, and when I bring you to see your granda to-morrow you musn't tell him about it. It's to be a surprise for him."

"Is the man coming to-night again," Tom asked excitedly.

"Sh, sh," she said.

She pushed the clothes around them and stood at the window looking down at the lamplighted street and its sweepings lying in little heaps awaiting the Corporation men to shovel them into their shambling cart. Her hand toyed with the tassel of the blind and it tocked against the pane.

"Don't pull down the blind, mother," Tom said.

"Close your eyes. If I hear another word out of you I'll come up and pull it down." Her hand rested on her cheek. The lamplight shone through the window and stretched a shadow of the sash on the ceiling. There was a shuffling step at the front door and presently a knock. It'll be Frank, she thought. She'd let him knock again so that a neighbour or two might get a look at him — it'd give them something more to talk about.

She went down and opened the door, helped him off with his overcoat and hung it on the rack in the hall. He smoothed his thick grey hair with his hand and took the newspaper out of his pocket.

"How are you this evening, Mary?" he said, putting his arm round her waist as they stepped into the parlour.

She threw back her head and smiled up at him; "The same as usual, Frank. The woman at the window they'll be calling me."

"Who'll be calling you the woman at the window?" he asked.

"The neighbours," she said, lighting the gas with a piece of twisted paper.

"The neighbours be damned. They'd find worse fault if you sat outside on the window-sill."

"I'm glad you think of them that way," she said. "Poor Peter, God rest him, always told me it was my imagination when I used to tell him how the neighbours were spying at me. He had always excuses for them because he was foreman in their factory, and was, in many ways, like one of themselves."

"You wouldn't like to spend all your days here?" he put in.

"I would not indeed. It'd be lovely to be in a place where you'd get fresh air and see flowers and trees growing," and she laughed. "That reminds me of a story Peter used to tell of a poor woman used to live next door to the factory and the only smell she got every day and every night was the oily smell from the wired factory-windows. And then one day that poor woman went to the country to spend a week and when she wakened in the morning she used to sniff and sniff and wonder what the smell was until some one told her it was fresh air."

"God above — that's a good one. Fresh air, she smelt. That poor woman wasn't about much in her life, I'd say," and he sat down in an arm-chair at the fire. "The old man will be fairly filling his lungs with fresh air these fine days, I'm thinking. Any word from him?"

"He's doing bravely," she said.

"He's a lucky man to have a place to go to in the country."

"All the same I miss him out of the house, Frank."

"The only thing I missed was the smell of his oul' pipe as I came in the door. He was too quiet — he hadn't a word to throw to a dog."

"Ah, Frank, if you knew him better you'd got on well together. He's an interesting man, and I often heard people say he knew more about country customs than you'd get in any book."

On the floor above them there was the pound of running feet and she stood, listening.

"One of them out of bed," she smiled, and when she went up the stairs he could hear her scolding and hooshing them.

"It was Tom," she said when she came into the parlour again. "He was looking out of the window."

"They have you tormented, Mary," he said, opening out his newspaper. "Why don't you pack them off to the country to their granda. The old man was fond of them and it'd do them a world of good to get to the country for awhile. There's nothing to beat the country for growing lads."

"I'd be lonely without them," she said, standing with one hand resting on the table and looking at him holding wide the wings of the paper.

"Lonely! Sure you'll have me."

She smiled and waited for him to add something more but he only turned back the wings of the paper, the stir of air shaking the flames in the fire.

"I'll wet the tea," she said, "I'll not be a tick."

When they were seated at the table and she was helping him to some salad there was the rumble of a cart outside, and then another pad of feet overhead and a laugh from the two boys.

"Aren't they the divils," she said.

"Wait and I'll go up to them, Mary."

"No, no, Frank, you might frighten them."

"Frighten them!"

"Well, I didn't mean frighten — I meant — how will I explain it."

"Aye, just how will you explain it! Look," and he shook his knife in the air, "them two boyos is playing on you. I know what I'm talking about and if you'd take my advice you'd pack them off to the country."

"Och, after all, Frank, they're only children and I often think if I could get one of the new houses at the outskirts of the city they'd get as much of the country that'd do them," and looking up at the ceiling she shouted: "Get into bed there, and go asleep or I'll go up with the strap."

In the street there was the scrape of a shovel on stone and then a cart knocking its way past the window. She smiled: "They were watching the council men lifting the sweepings off the street."

Frank said nothing. He drank what was left of his tea and rattled the cup down on the saucer with an air of finality. She stretched out her hand: "Another cup, Frank?"

"I've had enough," he said. She tried to coax him, and as she held out the teapot towards him he covered the mouth of his cup with his hand. "If I wanted it I'd take it," he tried to say casually.

She smiled at him: "You're an awful man!"

He lit a cigarette and turned round in his chair toward the fire. She, herself, stopped eating, and with her little finger toyed with the crumbs on the plate. A heavy constraint pressed upon her. She sighed.

"Do you know what I was thinking?" he said, flicking the ash of his cigarette into his cup. "What about coming for a walk on Sunday night now that the moon is full. A walk these nights would do you good and there'd be nobody to bother us."

She sat irresolute for awhile, manoeuvring the crumbs into a tiny heap and disarranging them again.

"Well, what do you say?" he pressed.

"I'd love to go, Frank, but it's impossible," and she motioned with her hand to the ceiling. "I've never left them in the house by themselves."

"So you care more about them than you do for the man that loves you!"

"Frank!" and she leaned over and touched his hand. "God knows what mischief they'd be up to."

"They're big enough and old enough to look after themselves for one night," he said, withdrawing his hand from hers.

"But look, Frank, if I met you outside the house it would be wrong and when I meet you inside the house it's wrong."

"How?"

"The neighbours!"

"So that's it! The neighbours!" he sneered. "You've the damned neighbours on the brain . . . . . I'll see you at the tram-depot at eight on Sunday night and we'll go up the Glen Road together." He turned completely round to the fire, took the tongs and lifted pieces of unlit coal and piled them on the handful of glow in the centre of the fire. There was a knock on the ceiling.

"At it again," he said, and opened his newspaper.

Another knock followed and Tom's voice rhyming: "Mother, John wants a drink of water. . . . John wants a drink of water . . . John wants a drink . . ."

Without a word she got up, went into the scullery for a cup of cold water, and while John was drinking it she stood silently by the bare window gazing down at the clean, moonlit street.

"If there's another word out of you I'll not bring you to see your granda to-morrow!" she said with sudden anger.

Frank was on his feet when she came back to the parlour.

"You're not going so soon?" she said.

"I promised my sisters I'd be home early to-night," and he looked into the mirror and combed back his hair.

"Stay for awhile," and she placed a hand on his shoulder.

"I can't," he said, and he stooped and kissed her, "Sure it won't be long till Sunday."

When he was at the door he looked at the moon skimming through the shreds of cloud: "Look at that for a night! And there we were stuck in the house."

"It's lovely," and she gave a half smile.

"Sunday at eight," he said. "Don't forget."

She nodded, and when he was gone she sat for awhile staring into the fire and twisting the wedding ring on her finger. Then realising that she was crying, she shrugged her shoulders, and lifting the cups and saucers on to a tray she carried them into the scullery to wash.

The following morning, Saturday, she was on her knees scrubbing the front doorstep before the smoke was rising from the chimney-pots in the neighbouring houses. She hummed to herself as she rubbed the soap on the scrubber and swept it in a half-circle in front of the door. Blinds were drawn in all the houses and a cat on a windowsill lay asleep beside two empty milk bottles. Nothing ruffled the chilly stillness of the morning except the streaky noise of the scrubber, the sharp rattle of her bucket, and the unchanging hum-hum of the factory at the top of the street. Steam rose from her fingers as she wrung out the cloth and got to her feet to wipe a few scribbles of chalk from the wall of the house. "It's always my house, they use as a blackboard," she said to herself, as she rubbed off a child's handwriting from the bricks. "Please God, it'll not be long till I leave this place for good." She came inside, put the boys' clean shirts to warm at the fire, and when she had made the breakfast she awakened them to pay their weekly visit to the workhouse.

As she walked down the street, John at one side of her and Tom at the other, she held her head high for she noticed the kitchen blinds being raised and a man in his shirt and trousers lifting a milk-bottle from a windowsill. Where is she off to at this time of the morning, they'd be saying — and God knows what answers they'd make for themselves. If they knew where the old man was they'd soon raise the colour to her cheeks and maybe get one of the children to chalk it up on the flagstones of the street or even on the wall of the house. Little they knew about where he was and she'd make sure they'd never know it. She always arrived early at the workhouse to have her visit over before the crowd of visitors thronged the main entrance gates.

This morning she was very silent as she got off the tram and made her way through the workhouse grounds with the autumn leaves hopping on the wind at her feet and her two boys tugging at her coat and asking to be allowed to run on in front. She spoke to them in a hushed voice and they, themselves, spoke back in the same way, quelled by the mysterious quiet of her manner. But when at last they came to the long flight of stairs that led to the ward they broke away from her, and when they entered the ward with its twelve aluminium-painted beds their granda saw them and he sat up in his red-flannel jacket and held out his hands to them as they ran to each side of his bed. "You're the early fellas," he said. "First in and first to go . . . And how are ye at all, at all," and he ruffled Tom's hair and then John's. Tom noticed an egg-stain on the red-jacket: "I see they've been stuffing eggs into you."

"Aw, aw, is that you, Tommy, my oul' codger!" said the granda.

"Don't be telling me you don't know me."

"I know you all right, my oul' jack-in-the-box. Come closer till I feel your muscles." And when he got Tom near him he rubbed his bristly chin against the boy's. "Do you feel the jag

of that! Will you tell Smith, the barber, to come up and give
me a decent shave. The fella, they've here, is no good and he
charges me a sixpence that I can ill afford."

The mother came into the ward, walking down between the
beds, looking neither to right nor left, and sat down on a chair
at the bedside, her handbag on her lap, a small brown parcel
dangling from her finger.

"My mother is going to get us a dog, granda," John was
saying.

The mother leaned across the bed and handed the parcel
to the old man: "There's a little tobacco and some tea," she
put in.

"Thank you kindly, girl," he said, and his hands fumbled to
open the knot of the parcel.

"You needn't open it — there's only an ounce of plug and a
quarter of tea in it."

"You're a good girl," he said, leaving the parcel on the table
at the head of the bed. "And how are you keeping since?"

"The same as usual," she said, keeping very erect on her
chair, her eyes now on the ivory buttons of his red jacket, and
now on his metal watch tied with a shoe-lace to the rail of his
bed.

"We're getting a dog soon," John said again.

"Stop chattering and let me talk to your granda," she said,
and she glanced to the foot of the ward and saw an old man
beckoning to them. "There's your old friend with the ear-phones
calling you. Away the both of you and hear the music." And
when they were gone, her father looked at her eyes without
flinching: "Anything strange?" he said.

"Nothing," she said, avoiding his eyes. "Are you keeping
well, yourself?"

"Too well, daughter, too well. If I'd pain or ache I might sleep for awhile and not feel the long days passing. But I'm too well, and there's nobody to talk to. Old Billdoe in the next bed is as deaf as a stone and the only comfort left me is to say my beads . . . Aw, girl, the doctor'll be sending me back to the body of the house — amongst the derelict, the nameless and the shameless. Would you not take me out, girl, till after Christmas and maybe in the spring of the year I might take a run down to the country and get a corner in some old neighbour's house."

She bent her head and smoothed out a crease in her skirt. A woman with a black shawl on her head shuffled in to visit Billdoe and she looked at Mary before sitting down. "That's a coul' mornin', Missus, the climb up them stairs hasn't left a grain of breath in me — not a damned happorth has it left." She let the shawl fall slack from her head and shouted into Billdoe's ear: "I've brought you some of Quinn's best sausages," and her voice rang through the ward. She tore the paper off the parcel and held out a clump of pork sausages: "They cost a bob a pound — they're the very best."

Billdoe took them in his hand and began eating a raw sausage.

"Give them to the nurse and she'll cook them for you," she shouted, trying to take them from him.

He stared at her with a stupid, affronted look: "I wouldn't give them God's daylight if I could keep it from them."

She arranged the shawl about her head and looked across at Mary: "There's the cross-grained article I've to deal with, Missus. But I fair miss him out of the house all the same — I do indeed."

Mary smiled thinly and patted the white quilt on the bed. Tom came running back: "Granda, I heard a drum and a fiddle on the ear-phones and the man said it came through the air from Paris."

"We'll be going soon," Mary said; and Tom ran back to get John.

"What's troubling you, girl?" and he leant close to her.

"Nothing," and she shook her head.

"There's something, girl, and if it's that Frank fella that's running after you, in God's name put him out of your head. He's no good, I tell you. He's no good," and he raised his voice.

"Hoosh, hoosh," she said. "The people will hear you."

He took her hand and she noticed how cold and thin it was. He lowered his voice: "I'm not thinking of myself, girl, God knows I'm not. I'm thinking of what's best for you and the two boys. But Frank — ah, God in heaven — he's not worth that!" and he snapped his fingers in the air. "He's not worth a dead match, so he's not. He's too settled in his ways and he'll not fit in with your ways and there'll be nothing but trouble."

"It's cold," she said, rubbing the backs of her hands and trying to ward off his talk.

"I never heard him speak a kind word to the children since the first day he darkened the door. I never seen him bring them a little toy or a wee bit of a sweet like many another. He has no nature in him, Mary. Ah, if you were thirty I'd tell you to marry again, but not to the likes of him. You're forty-three come next 12th December."

She flushed on hearing her age breathed so loudly, and she glanced at the shawled woman to see if she had heard.

"Who said I was going to marry again," she whispered and tried to smile.

"It'd be better for us all to get away to a place in the country where'd we live out our simple bit of life," he said.

"The country! I couldn't bury myself in the country — not after all I came through. And the boys' education?"

"They'll get education enough that'll do them. Look at me since I left the country fifty years ago. Look at me — ruined and flung to the side and not a place of my own to lay my head. And didn't I see the schoolmaster's son in the country and the policeman's son and the priest's nephew all going to big colleges and not one of them ever earned his bit of bread in his own country — out to foreign lands they went every man jack of them, and God knows if they're alive now or dead. Education! Is there one of them that wouldn't envy a man ploughing his own bit of land or talking about his own beasts in the fields? There is not! I had a good life at my own doorstep in the country and I didn't know I had it. I left it fifty years ago and now I know it! Blessed God in Heaven, I know it — and me shut between the black walls of a workhouse and my end coming."

"Shoosh, shoosh," Mary said.

Tom and John came running back and stared at Billdoe picking up the crumbs of raw sausage from the bed-clothes.

"You're back again," the granda sighed to them.

"We'll have to go now," Mary said, for she saw another visitor enter the ward — some day someone would be sure to see her if she weren't careful!

"Well, John," said the granda, "what about that big dog you were telling me about."

"He's getting no dog," the mother said. "Come now till we get home." And she stood up to take her leave.

"Wait now," said the granda, and he put his hand under the pillow and produced his purse tied with string. He gave them a penny each. "And, Tommy, don't forget to tell Smith to come up and give me a decent shave."

Mary shook her father's hand and he held on to it and looked up at her: "Night and day I'll pray you'll do the right thing." She smiled wanly down at him.

"Hurry up and get better," Tom said as they walked away.

At the door the boys turned round and waved to him and he waved back, and farther at the foot of the ward the man with the earphones was sitting up and waving too.

The mother walked quickly, and passing visitors with baskets she kept a handkerchief to her face, and held her head down in case some of them might know her. But once outside the main gates she cut down a nearby street and only then did she speak, scolding John for mentioning the dog.

"Will granda be home soon?" Tom said.

"I don't know," she said with obvious impatience.

"Will he be home for Christmas?" he persisted.

"I don't know. And what's more don't be giving granda's message to Smith. He's well enough shaved without sending a special man up for him."

Entering her own street she saw a few neighbours gossiping as usual at their doors. "Where's your granda if anybody asks you?" she warned the boys.

"He's away to the country for the good of his health," they answered.

"Quick now," she said, as she hurried up the street past the neighbours. At her own door she halted and though she held the key in her hand she pretended to search for it in her hand-bag. She'd just show the neighbours she wasn't a bit flustered about them. But out of the corner of her eye she saw that they had turned their backs to her. "Hm," she said aloud, and thought how they'd be gossiping about her now. To-morrow night she'd give them something else to talk about when she'd go for her walk with Frank and leave the boys for the first time in her life to mind the house. She opened the door and let the lads enter in front of her. After all they were big enough and old enough to stay alone in their bed for a few hours of a Sunday evening. She had them spoiled — there was no mistake about that. If they were anybody else's children in the street their mothers wouldn't give it a second thought.

She hung up her hat and coat in the hall and finding a smell of stale cigarette smoke coming from the parlour she went in and opened the window. On a chair she found a folded newspaper and her rolled-up *Woman's Notes*. She lifted the paper, and suddenly there came to her a sharp resentment against Frank: the way he refused the second cup of tea and the way he spread himself out before the fire. She paused; and then she saw herself mending and cooking for him, her boys with no education, and maybe her father dying a lonely death in the workhouse. "No," she said and she squeezed up the newspaper in a ball and flung it on the cold grate. "No, I'll not go to meet him to-morrow night! I'll not stir hand or foot out of the house. I'll see what he'll do then!"

When Sunday morning came her determination not to meet Frank had wavered, and throughout the day she was afraid to face the question whether or not she should go for the walk with him. If she stopped for a minute and put the question to herself she felt she'd give in to his arrangement, but rather than come to a decision she plunged herself into her work and tried to put him from her mind. She let the boys go up to the Park to gather chestnuts. After all if the worst came to the worst and she did go it'd be better if her boys were tired so that they'd settle down to sleep before she went out.

In the early evening when they had come back from their walk, hungry and tired, each had three glossy chestnuts which they held out to show her, and as she prepared their tea she watched them boring a hole in the chestnuts with a nail and threading a string through the hole. They began to play: Tom held his chestnut dangling from the end of a string and John whacked at it with his chestnut, and time and again they had to call to her to settle a dispute. But when they had taken their tea and were ready for bed she took the chestnuts from them and put them on the mantelpiece where they would take no harm until morning. Then she dressed and got ready to go out to meet Frank.

She went up to their room and was pleased to see the moon shining through the bare window: "Go asleep," she said, "I'll not be long till I'm back."

"Tell us a story," John pleaded, "and it will make us sleepy."

"I'll tell you one to-morrow night if you're good. If there's any knocks at the door don't open it, do you hear?"

"Are we going to get the dog?" John said.

"Yes."

"When's granda coming home?" Tom added.

"I don't know."

"Will he be home for Christmas?"

"We'll see . . . Go asleep now." And as she bent over to kiss them they smelt the warm thick perfume from her clothes.

They heard the front door close and her quick footsteps down the street. No neighbour had seen her, but once out of the street her steps lagged and she stopped under the light from a street-lamp and looked in her handbag to see if the key were safe. "I'm not doing right," she said to herself. "It's not right to leave them by themselves." She hesitated for a minute and then walked ahead. Frank shouldn't have asked her to do the like of this. Wasn't the comfort of the house and a fire better at this time of the year than rambling about the cold country roads. And what with his talk about the moon you'd think he was just a lad into long trousers. She should have laughed him out of that notion. Why must she be always playing a part and giving ear to his silly talk. Her father had said he's too settled in his ways — God knows he may be right, for there's something in what he said, now that she came to think about it.

She reached the road and just missed a tram, and while waiting for another a massive cloud trailed across the moon and scooped the light from the street. And then there came into her mind the sight of the boys' room, the moonlight slipping from it, leaving nothing only the slanting light from the street lamp and the shadow of the window-sash on the ceiling. A tram passed in the opposite direction and she saw the people within, warm and bright. The sky was black now, the moon entirely hidden. The night would be dark — what'd be the use of going, and it might rain and they'd have to turn back in any case. No, she needn't go. A tram came forward and she stepped away from the tram-stop and into the darkness. The car sped on. She crossed the road and hurried towards home. Up the street she went, her heels hard and clicking on the pavement. She put the key in the latch, and as she did so she heard the boys pounding up the stairs.

"Come back here!" she said, "Come back here!" Her voice was edged with anger. "Didn't you promise me not to get out of bed!" And she turned up the gaslight in the kitchen.

"We came down for a drink."

"What's that in your hand?"

"Chestnuts."

"I'll chestnut ye!" and in her anger she took the chestnuts and flung them into the fire.

They began to cry.

"That's for crying for nothing!" she said as she slapped each of them on the back of the hand. "Now go back and not another word out of you this night. You've my heart broken."

They ran from her, and she heard John sobbing as she hung up her hat and coat. She looked into the fire and tried to retrieve the chestnuts with the poker but the more she levered at them the more they disappeared into the red heart of the fire. She went to the foot of the stairs and called up to them: "Go asleep. I'll get you some chestnuts to-morrow."

She went into the parlour and put a match to the already prepared fire. She sat on a chair. It was a quarter past eight. He'd be sure to come when she didn't turn up. She went to the door. The darkness in the sky was loosening; she held out her hands, palms upward, in the hope of feeling spits of rain. But as she stood there the moon slid out and swung its shadows on roof and window.

She came into the parlour again, lifted her *Woman's Notes* but couldn't read it. Her head throbbed. She did the right thing in turning back — after all you'd never know what tricks Tom and John would be up to. A knock came to the door, and as she was tidying her hair before opening it the knock came again.

"I'm glad you came," she said, when Frank stepped in the hall. "Take off your coat."

"I'm not for staying. I'm foundered standing at the depot and searching every damned tram that came and turned."

She explained to him how she had gone out and turned home as she thought it would rain.

"Rain!" he said, "Rain — and the sky as smooth as silk. And why the blazes didn't you come up and tell me what you thought. Couldn't we've come back here if it had rained," and he sat on the edge of the table, swinging his hat in his hand.

"I never thought of that, Frank."

"No, you think of nothing only yourself and them two clips upstairs."

"Don't bring poor Tom and John into it."

"What about poor Frank," he said, and he got down from the table and buttoned his coat. "Well," he said, "are you going to come for the walk or are you not."

She sat on the arm-chair, rolling and unrolling her magazine. "Is it not too late?" she said meekly.

"Are you coming? — Yes or no?" he said, and the sharpness of his voice frightened her.

She turned a page in the magazine and then another. "Do you hear me — are you coming now or are you not?" Upstairs the boys startled by his voice began to cry and call to her. She drew herself erect from the chair: "No, Frank," she said slowly, "I'm not going to-night."

"All right," he said, and he put on his hat, and opened the front door to let himself out. In the stillness she heard her children crying, and she went up and lay down on top of the bed, her arms across them.

"What are you crying for? Go asleep."

"Is the man gone?" Tom said.

"He is and he'll never be back," and she combed her fingers through his hair.

There was a great stillness in the room and outside in the street where the moon was shining. She clenched and unclenched her hands to stifle the sob in her throat.

"When are you getting us the dog?" John asked her eagerly.

"Soon," she said.

"And will granda be home for Christmas?" Tom asked.

"He'll be out before it, before it," she said. "Not another word . . . Go asleep," and in the darkness as the tears flowed from her eyes she made no effort to stop them.

Pigeons

OUR Johnny kept pigeons, three white ones and a brown one that could tumble in the air like a leaf. They were nice pigeons, but they dirtied the slates and cooed so early in the morning that my Daddy said that someday he would wring their bloody necks. That is a long while ago now, for we still have the pigeons, but Johnny is dead; he died for Ireland.

Whenever I think of our Johnny I always think of Saturday. Nearly every Saturday night he had something for me, maybe sweets, a toy train, a whistle, or glass marbles with rainbows inside them. I would be in bed when he'd come home; I always tried to keep awake, but my eyes wouldn't let me — they always closed tight when I wasn't thinking. We both slept together in the wee back room, and when Johnny came up to bed he always lit the gas, the gas that had no mantle. If he had something for me he would shake me and say: "Frankie, Frankie, are you asleep?" My eyes would be very gluey and I would rub them with my fists until they would open in the gaslight. For a long while I would see gold needles sticking out of the flame, then they would melt away and the gas become like a pansy leaf with a blue heart. Johnny would be standing beside the bed and I would smile all blinky at him. Maybe he'd stick a sweet in my mouth, but if I hadn't said my prayers he'd lift me out on to the cold, cold floor. When I would be jumping in again in my shirt tails, he would play whack at me and laugh if he got me. Soon he would climb into bed and tell me about the ice-cream shops, and the bird-shop that had funny pigeons and rabbits and mice in the window. Someday he was going to bring me down the town and buy me a black and white mouse, and a custard bun full of ice-cream. But he'll never do it now because he died for Ireland.

On Saturdays, too, I watched for him at the backdoor when he was coming from work. He always came over the waste ground, because it was the shortest. His dungarees would be all shiny, but they hadn't a nice smell. I would pull them off him, and he would lift me on to his shoulder, and swing me round and round until my head got light and the things in the kitchen went up and down. My Mammie said he had me spoilt. He always gave me pennies on Saturday, two pennies, and I bought a licorice pipe with one penny and kept the other for Sunday. Then he would go into the cold scullery to wash his black hands and face; he would stand at the sink, scrubbing and scrubbing and singing "The Old Rusty Bridge by the Mill", but if you went near him he'd squirt soap in your eye. After he had washed himself, we would get our Saturday dinner, the dinner with the sausages because it was pay-day. Johnny used to give me a bit of his sausages, but if my Mammie saw me she'd slap me for taking the bite out of his mouth. It was a long, long wait before we went out to the yard to the pigeons.

The pigeon-shed was on the slates above the closet. There was a ladder up to it, but Johnny wouldn't let me climb for fear I'd break my neck. But I used to climb up when he wasn't looking. There was a great flutter and flapping of wings when Johnny would open the trap-door to let them out. They would fly out in a line, brownie first and the white ones last. We would

lie on the waste ground at the back of our street watching them
fly. They would fly round and round, rising higher and higher
each time. Then they would fly so high we would blink our
eyes and lose them in the blue sky. But Johnny always found
them first. "I can see them, Frankie," he would say. "Yonder
they are. Look! above the brickyard chimney." He would put
his arm around my neck, pointing with his outstretched hand.
I would strain my eyes, and at last I would see them, their wings
flashing in the sun as they turned towards home. They were
great fliers. But brownie would get tired and he would tumble
head over heels like you'd think he was going to fall. The white
ones always flew down to him, and Johnny would go wild.
"He's a good tumbler, but he won't let the others fly high. I
think I'll sell him." He would look at me, plucking at the grass,
afraid to look up. "Ah, Frankie," he would say, "I won't sell
him. Sure I'm only codding." All day we would sit, if the weather
was good, watching our pigeons flying, and brownie doing
somersaults. When they were tired they would light on the
blue slates, and Johnny would throw corn up to them. Saturday
was a great day for us and for our pigeons, but it was on
Saturday that Johnny died for Ireland.

We were lying, as usual, at the back, while the pigeons were
let out for a fly round. It was a lovely sunny day. Every house
had clothes out on the lines, and the clothes were fluttering in
the breeze. Some of the neighbours were sitting at their back-
doors, nursing babies or darning socks. They weren't nice
neighbours for they told the rent-man about the shed on the
slates, and he made us pay a penny a week for it. But we didn't
talk much to them, for we loved our pigeons, and on that lovely
day we were splitting our sides laughing at the way brownie
was tumbling, when a strange man in a black hat and burberry

coat came near us. Johnny jumped up and went to meet him.
I saw them talking, with their heads bent towards the ground,
and then the strange man went away. Johnny looked very sad
and he didn't laugh at brownie any more. He gave me the
things out of his pockets, a penknife, a key, and a little blue
note-book with its edges all curled. "Don't say anything to
Mammie. Look after the pigeons, Frankie, until I come back.
I won't be long." He gave my hand a tight squeeze, then he
walked away without turning round to wave at me.

All that day I lay out watching the pigeons, and when I got
tired I opened the note-book. It had a smell of fags and there
was fag-dust inside it. I could read what he had written down:

Corn	2-6d
Club	6d
3 Pkts. Woodbine	6d
Frankie	2d

He had the same thing written down on a whole lot of pages;
if he had been at school he would have got slapped for wasting
the good paper. I put the note-book in my pocket when my
Mammie called me for my tea. She asked me about Johnny
and I told her he wouldn't be long until he was back. Then
it got late. The pigeons flew off the slates and into the shed, and
still Johnny didn't come back.

It came on night. My sisters were sent out to look for him.
My daddy came home from work. We were all in now, my two
sisters and Mammy and Daddy, everyone except Johnny.
Daddy took out his pipe with the tin lid, but he didn't light it.
We were all quiet, but my mother's hands would move from
her lap to her chin, and she was sighing. The kettle began hum-

ming and shuffling the lid about, and my Daddy lifted it off the
fire and placed it on the warm hob. The clock on the mantelpiece chimed eleven and my sisters blessed thmeselves — it got
a soul out of Purgatory when you did that. They forgot all about
my bed-time and I was let stay up though my eyes felt full of
sand. The rain was falling. We could hear it slapping in the
yard and trindling down the grate. It was a blowy night for
someone's back-door was banging, making the dogs bark. The
newspapers that lay on the scullery floor to keep it clean began
to crackle up and down with the wind till you'd have thought
there was a mouse under them. A bicycle bell rang in the
street outside our kitchen window and it made Mammie jump.
Then a motor rattled down, shaking the house and the vases
on the shelf. My Daddy opened the scullery door and went into
the yard. The gas blinked and a coughing smell of a chimney
burning came into the kitchen. I'm sure it was Mrs. Ryan's. She
always burned hers on a wet night. If the peelers caught her
she'd be locked in jail, for you weren't allowed to burn your
own chimney.

I wish Daddy would burn ours. It was nice to see him putting
the bunch of lighted papers on the yard-brush and sticking
them up the wide chimney. The chimney would roar, and if
you went outside you'd see lines of sparks like hot wires coming
out and the smoke bubbling over like lemonade in a bottle.
But he wouldn't burn it to-night, because we were waiting on
Johnny.

"Is there any sign of him?" said Mammie, when Daddy came
in again.

"None yet; but he'll be all right; he'll be all right. We'll say
the prayers, and he'll be in before we're finished."

We were just ready to kneel when a knock came to the back-

door. It was a very dim knock and we all sat still, listening.
"That's him, now," said Daddy, and I saw my mother's face
brightening. Daddy went into the yard and I heard the stiff bar
on the door opening and feet shuffling. "Easy now: Easy now,"
said someone. Then Daddy came in, his face as white as a sheet.
He said something to Mammie. "Mother of God it isn't true —
it isn't!" she said. Daddy turned and sent me up to bed.

Up in the wee room I could see down into the yard. The light
from the kitchen shone into it and I saw men with black hats
and the rain falling on them like little needles, but I couldn't
see our Johnny. I looked up at the shed on the slates, the rain
was melting down its sides, and the wet felt was shining like
new boots. When I looked into the yard again, Daddy was
bending over something. I got frightened and went into my
sisters' room. They were crying and I cried, too, while I sat
shivering in my shirt and my teeth chattering. "What's wrong?"
I asked. But they only cried and said: "Nothing, son. Nothing.
Go to sleep, Frankie, like a good little boy." My big sister put me
into her bed, and put the clothes around me and stroked my
head. Then she lay on the top of the bed beside me, and I
could feel her breathing heavily on my back. Outside it was
still blowy for the wind was kicking an empty salmon-tin
which rattled along the street. For a long time I listened to the
noises the wind made, and then I slept.

In the morning when I opened my eyes I wondered at finding myself in my sisters' room. It was very still: the blinds were
down and the room was full of yellow light. I listened for the
sound of plates, a brush scrubbing, or my big sister singing.
But I heard nothing, neither inside the house nor outside it.
I remembered about last night, my sisters crying because our
Johnny didn't come home. I sat up in bed; I felt afraid because

the house was strange, and I got out and went into the wee back room.

The door was open and there was yellow light in it, too, and the back of the bed had white cloth and I couldn't see over it. Then I saw my Mammie in the room sitting on a chair. She stretched out her arms and I ran across and knelt beside her, burying my face in her lap. She had on a smooth, black dress, and I could smell the camphor balls off it, the smell that kills the moths, the funny things with no blood and no bones that eat holes in your jersey. There were no holes in Mammie's dress. She rubbed my head with her hands and said: "You're the only boy I have now." I could hear her heart thumping very hard, and then she cried, and I cried and cried, with my head down on her lap. "What's wrong, Mammie?" I asked, looking up at her wet eyes. "Nothing, darling: nothing, pet. He died for Ireland." I turned my head and looked at the bed. Johnny was lying on the white bed in a brown dress. His hands were pale and they were joined around his rosary beads, and a big crucifix between them. There was a big lump of wadding at the side of his head and wee pieces up his nose. I cried more and more, and then my Mammie made me put on my clothes, and go downstairs for my breakfast.

All that day my Mammie stayed in the room to talk to the people that came to see our Johnny. And all the women shook hands with Mammie and they all said the same thing: "I'm sorry for your trouble, but he died for his country." They knelt beside the white bed and prayed, and then sat for awhile looking at Johnny, and speaking in low whispers. My sisters brought them wine and biscuits, and some of them cried when they were taking it, dabbing their eyes with their handkerchiefs or the tails of their shawls. Mrs. McCann came and she got wine, too, though she had told the rent man about the shed on the slates and we had to pay a penny a week. I was in the wee room when she came, and I saw her looking at the lighted candles and the flowers on the table, and up at the gas that had no mantle. But she couldn't see it because my big sister had put white paper over it, and she had done the same with the four brass knobs on the bed. She began to sniff and sniff and my Mammie opened the window without saying anything. The blind began to snuffle in and out, the lighted candles to waggle, and the flowers to smell. We could hear the pigeons cooing and flapping in the shed, and I could see at the back of my eyes, their necks fattening and their feathers bristling like a dog going to fight. It's well Daddy didn't hear them or he might have wrung their necks.

At night the kitchen was crammed with men and women, and many had to sit in the cold scullery. Mrs. Ryan, next door, lent us her chairs for the people to sit on. There was lemonade and biscuits and tea and porter. Some of the men, who drank black porter, gave me pennies, and they smoked and talked all night. The kitchen was full of smoke and it made your eyes sting. One man told my Daddy he should be a proud man, because Johnny had died for the Republic. My Daddy blinked his eyes when he heard this, and he got up and went into the yard for a long time.

The next day was the funeral. Black shiny horses with their mouths all suds, and silver buckles on their straps, came trotting into the street. All the wee lads were looking at themselves in the glossy backs of the cabs where you could see yourself all fat and funny like a dwarf. I didn't play because Johnny was dead and I had on a new, dark suit. Jack Byrne was out

playing and he told me that we had only two cabs and that
there were three cabs at his Daddy's funeral. There were crowds
of peelers in the street, some of them talking to tall, red-faced
men with overcoats and walking sticks.

Three men along with my Daddy carried the yellow coffin
down the stairs. There was a green, white, and gold flag over
it. But a thin policeman, with a black walking stick and black
leggins, pulled the flag off the coffin when it went into the
street. Then a girl snatched the flag out of the peeler's hands
and he turned all pale. At the end of our street there were more
peelers and every one wore a harp with a crown on his cap.
Brother Gabriel used to fairly wallop us in school if we drew
harps with crowns on them. One day we told him the peelers
wore them on their caps. "Huh!" he said, "The police! the
police! They don't love their country. They serve England.
England, my boys! The England that chased our people to
live in the damp bogs! The England that starved our ancestors
till they had to eat grass and nettles by the roadside. And our
poor priests had to say Mass out on the cold mountains! No,
my dear boys, never draw a harp with a crown on it!" And
then he got us to write in our books:

"Next to God I love thee
Dear Ireland, my native land!"

"It's a glorious thing," he said, "to die for Ireland, to die for
Ireland!" His voice got very shaky when he said this and he
turned his back and looked into the press. But Brother Gabriel
is not in the school now; if he was he'd be good to me, because
our Johnny died for Ireland.

The road to the cemetery was lined with people. Little boys

that were at my school lifted a fringe of hair when the coffin passed. The trams were stopped in a big, long line — it was nice to see so many at one look. Outside the gates of the graveyard there was an armoured car with no one peeping his head out. Inside it was very still and warm with the sun shining. With my Daddy I walked behind the carried coffin and it smelt like the new seats in the chapel. The crowds of people were quiet. You could hear the cinders on the path squanching as we walked over them, and now and again the horses snorting.

I began to cry when I saw the deep hole in the ground and the big castles of red clay at the side of it. A priest, with a purple sash round his neck, shovelled a taste of clay on the coffin and it made a hard rattle that made me cry sore. Daddy had his head bowed and there were tears in his eyes, but they didn't run down his cheeks like mine did. The priest began to pray, and I knew I'd never see Johnny again, never, never, until I'd die and go to Heaven if I kept good and didn't say bad words and obeyed my Mammie and my Daddy. But I wouldn't like Daddy to tell me to give away the pigeons. When the prayers were over a tall man with no hat and a wee moustache stood beside the grave and began to talk. He talked about our Johnny being a soldier of the Republic, and, now and then, he pointed with his finger at the grave. As soon as he stopped talking we said the Rosary, and all the people went away. I got a ride back in a black cab with my Daddy and Uncle Pat and Uncle Joe. We stopped at "The Bee Hive" and they bought lemonade for me and porter for the cab driver. And then we went home.

I still have the pigeons and big Tom Duffy helps me to clean the shed and let them out to fly. Near night I give them plenty of corn so that they'll sleep long and not waken Daddy in the morning. When I see them fattening their necks and cooing I clod them off the slates.

Yesterday I was lying on the waste ground watching the pigeons and Daddy came walking towards me smoking his pipe with the tin lid. I tried to show him the pigeons flying through the clouds. He only looked at them for a minute and turned away without speaking, and now I'm hoping he won't wring their necks.

Father Christmas

"WILL you do what I ask you?" his wife said again, wiping the crumbs off the newspaper which served as a table-cloth. "Wear your hard hat and you'll get the job."

He didn't answer her or raise his head. He was seated on the dilapidated sofa lacing his boots, and behind him tumbled two of his children, each chewing a crust of bread. His wife paused, a hand on her hip. She glanced at the sleety rain falling into the backyard, turned round, and threw the crumbs into the fire.

"You'll wear it, John — won't you?"

Again he didn't answer though his mind was already made up. He strode into the scullery and while he washed himself she took an overcoat from a nail behind the kitchen door, brushed it vigorously, gouging out the specks of dirt with the nose of the brush. She put it over the back of a chair and went upstairs for his hard hat.

"I'm a holy show in that article," he said, when she was handing him the hat and helping him into the overcoat. "I'll be a nice ornament among the other applicants! I wish you'd leave me alone!"

"You look respectable anyhow. I could take a fancy for you all over again," and she kissed him playfully on the side of the cheek.

"If I don't get the job you needn't blame me. I've done all
you asked — every mortal thing."

"You'll get it all right — never you fear. I know what I'm talking about."

He hurried out of the street in case some of the neighbours
would ask him if he were going to a funeral, and when he
had taken his place in the line of young men who were all
applying for the job of Father Christmas in the Big Store
he was still conscious of the bowler hat perched on top of
his head. He was a timid little man and he tried to crouch
closer to the wall and make himself inconspicuous amongst
that group of grey-capped men. The rain continued to fall
as they waited for the door to open and he watched the
drops clinging to the peaks of their caps, swelling and
falling to the ground.

"If he had a beard we could all go home," he heard someone say, and he felt his ears reddening, aware that the remark
was cast at him. But later when he was following the Manager up the brass-lipped stairs, after he had got the job, he
dwelt on the wisdom of his wife and knew that the hat had
endowed him with an air of shabby respectability.

"Are you married?" the Manager had asked him, looking
at the nervous way he turned the hat in his hand. "And have
you any children?" He had answered everything with a meek
smile and the Manager told him to stand aside until he had
interviewed, as a matter of form, the rest of the applicants.

And then the interviews were quickly over, and when the
Manager and John were mounting the stairs he saw a piece
of caramel paper sticking to the Manager's heel. Down a long
aisle they passed with rows of counters at each side and shop-
pers gathered round them. And though it was daylight outside,

the electric lights were lit, and through the glare there arose a buzz of talk, the rattle of money, and the warm smell of new clothes and perfume and confectionery — all of it entering John's mind in a confused and dreamy fashion for his eye was fastened on the caramel paper as he followed respectfully after the Manager. Presently they emerged on a short flight of stairs where a notice – PRIVATE — on trestles straddled across it. The Manager lifted it ostentatiously to the side, ushered John forward with a sweep of his arm, and replaced the notice with mechanical importance.

"Just a minute," said John, and he plucked the caramel paper from the Manager's heel, crumpled it between his fingers, and put it in his pocket.

They entered the quiet seclusion of a small room that had a choking smell of dust and cardboard boxes. The Manager mounted a step-ladder, and taking a large box from the top shelf looked at something written on the side, slapped the dust off it against his knee, and broke the string.

"Here," he said, throwing down the box. "You'll get a red cloak in that and a white beard." He sat on the top rung of the ladder and held a false face on the tip of his finger: "Somehow I don't think you'll need this. You'll do as you are. Just put on the beard and whiskers."

"Whatever you say," smiled John, for he always tried to please people.

Another box fell at his feet: "You'll get a pair of top boots in that!" The Manager folded the step-ladder, and daintily picking pieces of fluff from his sleeves he outlined John's duties for the day and emphasised that after closing-time he'd have to make up parcels for the following day's sale.

Left alone John breathed freely, took off his overcoat and

hung it at the back of the door, and for some reason whenever he crossed the floor he did so on his tiptoes. He lifted the red cloak that was trimmed with fur, held it in his outstretched arms to admire it, and squeezed the life out of a moth that was struggling in one of the folds. Chips of tinsel glinted on the shoulders of the cloak and he was ready to flick them off when he decided it was more Christmassy-looking to let them remain on. He pulled on the cloak, crossed on tiptoes to a looking-glass on the wall and winked and grimaced at himself, sometimes putting up the collar of the cloak to enjoy the warm touch of the fur on the back of his neck. He attached the beard and the whiskers, spitting out one or two hairs that had strayed into his mouth.

"The very I-T," he said, and caught the beard in his fist and waggled it at his reflection in the mirror. "Hello, Santa!" he smiled, and thought of his children and how they would laugh to see him togged up in this regalia. "I must tell her to bring them down some day," and he gave a twirl on his toes, making a heap of paper rustle in the corner.

He took off his boots, looked reflectively at the broken sole of each and pressed his thumb into the wet leather: "Pasteboard — nothing else!" he said in disgust, and threw them on the heap of brown paper. He reached for the top boots that were trimmed with fur. They looked a bit on the small side. With some difficulty he squeezed his feet into them. He walked across the floor, examining the boots at each step; they were very tight for him, but he wasn't one to complain, and, after all, the job was only for the Christmas season and they'd be sure to stretch with the wearing.

When he was fully dressed he made his way down the stairs, lifted his leg over the trestle with the name PRIVATE and presented himself on one of the busy floors. A shop-girl, hesitating before striking the cash-register, smiled over at him. His face burned. Then a little girl plucked her mother's skirt and called, "Oh, Mammy, there's Daddy Christmas!" With his hands in his wide sleeves he stood in a state of nervous perplexity till the shop-girl, scratching her head with the tip of her pencil, shouted jauntily: "First Floor, Santa Claus, right on down the stairs!" He stumbled on the stairs because of the tight boots and when he halted to regain his composure he felt the blood hammering in his temples and he wished now that he hadn't listened to his wife and worn his hard hat. She was always nagging at him, night, noon and morning, and he doing his damned best!

On the first floor the Manager beckoned him to a minia-ture house — a house painted in imitation brick, snow on the eaves, a door which he could enter by stooping low, and a chimney large enough to contain his head and shoulders, and inside the house stacks of boxes neatly piled, some in blue paper and others in pink.

The Manager produced a hand-bell. "You stand here," said the Manager, placing himself at the door of the house. "Ring your bell a few times — like this. Then shout in a loud, commanding voice: 'Roll up now! Blue for the Boys, and Pink for the Girls.'" And he explained that when business was slack, he was to mount the ladder, descend the chimney, and bring up the parcels in that manner, but if there was a crowd he was just to open the door and shake hands with each child before presenting the boxes. They were all the same price — a shilling each.

For the first ten minutes or so John's voice was weak and self-conscious and the Manager, standing a short distance away, ordered him to raise his voice a little louder: "You must attract attention — that's what you're paid for. Try it once again."

"Blue for the Boys, and Pink for the Girls!" shouted John, and he imagined all the buyers at the neighbouring counters had paused to listen to him. "Blue for the Boys, and Pink for the Girls!" he repeated, his eye on the Manager who was judging him from a distance. The Manager smiled his approval and then shook an imaginary bell in the air. John suddenly remembered about the bell in his hand and he shook it vigorously, but a shop-girl tightened up her face at him and he folded his fingers over the skirt of the bell in order to muffle the sound. He gained more confidence, but as his nervousness decreased he became aware of the tight boots imprisoning his feet, and occasionally he would disappear into his little house and catching the sole of each in turn he would stretch them across his knee.

But the children gave him no peace, and with his head held genially to the side, if the Manager were watching him, he would smile broadly and listen with affected interest to each child's demand.

"Please, Santa Claus, bring me a tricycle at Christmas and a doll's pram for Angela."

"I'll do that! Everything you want," said Father Christmas expansively, and he patted the little boy on the head with gentle dignity before handing him a blue parcel. But when he raised his eyes to the boy's mother she froze him with a look. "I didn't think you would have any tricycles this year," she said. "I thought you were only making wooden trains."

"Oh, yes! No, yes. Not at all! Yes, of course, I'll get you a nice wooden train," Father Christmas turned to the boy in his confusion. "If you keep good I'll have a lovely train for you."

"I don't want an oul train. I want a tricycle," the boy whimpered, clutching his blue-papered parcel.

"I couldn't make any tricycles this year," consoled Father Christmas. "My reindeers was sick and three of them died on me."

The boy's mother smiled and took him by the hand. "Now, pet, didn't I tell you Santa had no tricycles? You better shout up the chimney for something else — a nice game or a wooden train."

"I don't want an oul game — I want a tricycle," he cried, and jigged his feet.

"You'll get a warm ear if you're not careful. Come on now and none of your nonsense. And Daddy Christmas after giving you a nice box, all for yourself."

Forcibly she led the boy away and John, standing with his hands in his sleeves, felt the prickles of sweat on his forehead and resolved to promise nothing to the children until he had got the cue from the parents.

As the day progressed he climbed up the ladder and down the chimney, emerging again with his arms laden with parcels. His feet tortured him and when he glanced at the boots every wrinkle in the leather was smoothed away. He couldn't continue like this all day; it would drive him mad.

"Roll up!" he bawled. "Roll up! Blue for the Pinks and Boys for the Girls! Roll up, I say. Blue for the Pinks and Boys for the Girls." Then he stopped and repeated the same mistake before catching himself up. And once more he clanged the bell with subdued ferocity till its sound drowned the jingle of the cash-registers and the shop-girls had to shout to be heard.

At one o'clock he wearily climbed the stairs to the quiet room, where dinner was brought to him on a tray. He took off his boots and gazed sympathetically at his crushed toes. He massaged them tenderly, and when he had finished his dinner he pared his corns with a razor blade he had bought at one of the counters. He now squeezed his bare feet into the boots, walked across the room, and sat down again, his face twisted with despair. "Why do I always give in to that woman," he said aloud to himself. "I've no strength — no power to stand up and shout in her face: 'No, no, no! I'll go my own way in my own time!'" He'd let her know to-night the agony he suffered, and his poor feet gathered up all day like a rheumatic fist.

Calmed after this outburst, and reassuring himself that the job was only for three weeks, he gave a whistle of forced satisfaction, brushed the corn-parings off the chair, and went off to stand outside the little house with its imitation snow on the chimney.

The afternoon was the busiest time, and he was glad to be able to stand at the door like a human being and hand out the parcels, instead of ascending and descending the ladder like a trained monkey. When the children crowded too close to him he kept them at arm's length in case they'd trample on his feet. But he always managed to smile as he watched them shaking their boxes or tearing holes in the paper in an effort to guess what was inside. And the parents smiled too when they looked at him wagging his finger at the little girls and promising them dolls at Christmas if they would go to bed early, eat their porridge and stop biting their nails. But before closing time a woman was back holding an untidy parcel. "That's supposed to be for a boy," she said peevishly.

"There's a rubber doll in it and my wee boy has cried his eyes out ever since."

"I'm just new to the job," Father Christmas apologised. "It'll never occur again." And he tossed the parcel into the house and handed the woman a new one.

At the end of his day he had gathered from the floor a glove with a hole in one finger, three handkerchiefs, a necklace of blue beads, and a child's handbag containing a halfpenny and three tram-tickets. When he was handing them to the Manager he wondered if he should complain about the boots, but the tired look on the Manager's face and his reminder about staying behind to make up parcels discouraged him.

For the last time he climbed the stairs, took off his boots and flung them from him, and as he prepared the boxes he padded about the cool floor in his bare feet, and to ensure that he wouldn't make a mistake he arranged, at one side of the room, the contents for the girls' boxes: dolls, shops, pages of transfers, story books, and crayons; and at the opposite side of the room the toys for the boys: ludo, snakes and ladders, blow football, soldiers, cowboy outfits, and wooden whistles. And as he parcelled them neatly and made loops in the twine for the children's fingers he decided once again to tell his wife to bring his own kids along and he'd have special parcels prepared for them.

On his way out of the Store the floors were silent and deserted, the counters humped with canvas covers, and the little house looking strangely real now under a solitary light. A mouse nibbling at something on the floor scurried off between an alleyway in the counters, and on the ground floor two women were sweeping up the dust and gossiping loudly.

The caretaker let him out by a side door, and as he walked off in the rain through the lamp-lighted streets he put up the collar of his coat and avoided the puddles as best he could. A sullen resentment seized his heart and he began to drag from the corners of his mind the things that irritated him. He thought they should have given him his tea before he left, or even a bun and a glass of milk, and he thought of his home and maybe the fine tea his wife would have for him, and a good fire in the grate and the kids in bed. He walked more quickly. He passed boys eating chip potatoes out of a newspaper, and he stole a glance at Joe Raffo's chip-shop and the cloud of steam rolling through the open door into the cold air. The smell maddened him. He plunged his hands into his pockets and fiddled with a button, bits of hard crumbs, and a sticky bit of caramel paper. He took out the caramel paper and threw it on the wet street.

He felt cheated and discontented with everything; and the more he thought of the job the more he blamed his wife for all the agony he had suffered throughout the day. She couldn't leave him alone — not for one solitary minute could she let him have a thought of his own or come to a decision of his own. She must be for ever interfering, barging in, and poking into his business. He was a damned fool to listen to her and to don a ridiculous hard hat for such a miserable job. Father Christmas and his everlasting smile! He'd smile less if he had to wear a pair of boots three sizes too small for him. It was a young fella they wanted for the job — somebody accustomed to standing for hours at a street corner and measuring the length of his spits on the kerb. And then the ladder! That was the bloody limit! Up and down, down and up, like a squirrel in a cage, instead of giving you a stick and a chair where you could sit and really look like an old man. When he'd get home he'd let his wife know what she let him in for. It would lead to a row between them, and when that happened she'd go about for days flinging his meals on the table and belting the kids for sweet damn-all. He'd have to tell her — it was no use suffering devil's torture and saying nothing about it. But then, it's more likely than not she'd put on her hat and coat and go down to the Manager in the morning and complain about the boots, and then he might lose the job, bad and all as it was. Och, he'd say nothing — sure, bad temper never got you anywhere!

He stepped into a puddle to avoid a man's umbrella and when he felt the cold splash of water up the leg of his trousers his anger surged back again. He'd tell her all. He'd soon take the wind out of her sails and her self-praise about the hat! He'd tell her everything.

He hurried up the street and at the door of his house he let down the collar of his coat and shook the rain off his hat. He listened for a minute and heard the children shouting. He knocked, and the three of them pounded to the door to open it.

"It's Daddy," they shouted, but he brushed past them without speaking.

His wife was washing the floor in the kitchen and as she wrung the cloth into the bucket and brushed back her hair with the back of her hand she looked at him with a bright smile.

"You got it all right?"

"Why aren't the children in bed?"

"I didn't expect you home so soon."

"Did you think I was a bus conductor!"

She noticed the hard ring in his voice. She rubbed the soap on the scrubber and hurried to finish her work, making great whorls and sweeps with the cloth. She took off her dirty apron, and as she washed and dried her hands in the scullery she glanced in at him seated on the sofa, his head resting on his hands, the three children waiting for him to speak to them. "It was the hat," she said to herself. "It was the hat did the trick."

"Come on now and up to bed quickly," and she clapped her hands at the children.

"But you have to wash our legs in the bucket."

"You'll do all right for to-night. Your poor father's hungry after his hard day's work." And as she pulled off a jersey she held it in her hand and gave the fire a poke under the kettle. John stared into the fire and when he raised his foot there was a damp imprint left on the tiles. She handed him a pair of warm socks from the line and a pair of old slippers that she had made for him out of pasteboard and a piece of velours.

"I've a nice bit of steak for your tea," she said. "I'll put on the pan when I get these ones into their beds."

He rubbed his feet and pulled on the warm socks. It was good that she hadn't the steak fried and lying as dry as a stick in the oven. When all was said and done, she had some sense in her head.

The children began to shout up the chimney telling Santa Claus what they wanted for Christmas, and when they knelt to say their prayers they had to thank God for sending their Daddy a good job. John smiled for the first time since he came into the house and he took the youngest on his knee. "You'll get a doll and a pram for Christmas," he said, "and Johnny will get a wooden train with real wheels and Pat — what will we get him?" And he remembered putting a cowboy's outfit into one of the boxes. "A cowboy's outfit — hat and gun."

His wife had put the pan on the fire and already the steak was frizzling. "Don't let that pan burn till I come down again. I'll not be a minute."

He heard her put the kids to bed, and in a few minutes she was down again, a fresh blouse on her and a clean apron.

She poured out his tea and after he had taken a few mouthfuls he began to tell her about the crowd of applicants and about the fellow who shouted: "We'd better all go home," when he had seen him in the hat.

"He was jealous — that's what was wrong with him!" she said. "A good clout on the ear he needed."

He told her about the Manager, the handbell, the blue and pink parcels, the little house, and the red cloak he had to wear. Then he paused, took a drink of tea, cut a piece of bread into three bits, and went on eating slowly.

"It's well you took my advice and wore the hat," she said brightly. "I knew what I was talking about. And you look so — so manly in it." She remembered about the damp stain on the floor, and she lifted his boots off the fender and looked at the broken soles. "They're done," she said, "that's the first call in your wages at the end of the week."

He got up from the table and sat near the fire. She handed him his pipe filled with tobacco, and as she washed the dishes in the scullery she would listen to the little pouts he made while he smoked. Now and again she glanced in at him, at the contented look on his face and the steam rising from his boots on the fender.

She took off her apron, tidied her hair at the looking-glass, and powdered her face. She stole across the floor to him as he sat staring into the fire. Quietly she took the pipe from his lips and put it on the mantelpiece. She smiled at him and he smiled back, and as she stooped to kiss him he knew that he would say nothing to her now about the tight boots.